PRAISE FOR *WE SPREAD*

"Hypnotic . . . With tenderness and mastery, [Reid] offers us great insights on the nature of aging and the vertiginous experience of being human."

Alexandra Kleeman, author of *Something New Under the Sun*

"Reid masterfully gets into the psyche of his characters and readers all at once. What a gift."

Alma Har'el, director of *Bombay Beach* and *Honey Boy*

PRAISE FOR *FOE*

National Bestseller

A *Globe and Mail* Favorite Book of 2018 • A *Chatelaine* Best Book of 2018 • Winner of the 2020–2021 MacEwan Book of the Year

"Reads like a house on fire, and is almost impossible not to finish in one sitting. . . . An otherworldly hothouse of introversion and fantasy."

Toronto Star

"Reid just might be the most exciting and excitingly unclassifiable author working in Canadian fiction today."

The Globe and Mail

"Reid is a master storyteller with a knack for absorbing prose."

Los Angeles Review of Books

"I couldn't put it down. It infected my dreams. A creepy and brilliant book."

Zoe Whittall, bestselling author of *The Spectacular*

PRAISE FOR *I'M THINKING OF ENDING THINGS*

National Bestseller

Now a critically acclaimed Netflix film • A *Globe and Mail* Best Book • An Amazon Editors' Top 20 of 2016 • An NPR Best Book of 2016 • A 49th Shelf Book of the Year

"An ingeniously twisted nightmare road trip through the fragile psyches of two young lovers. My kind of fun!"

Charlie Kaufman, director of *I'm Thinking of Ending Things*

"An unnerving exploration of identity, regret, and longing. Delightfully frightening."

The Globe and Mail

"An addictive metaphysical investigation into the nature of identity, one which seduces and horrifies in equal measure."

Heather O'Neill, author of *Lullabies for Little Criminals* and *The Lonely Hearts Hotel*

"A deviously smart, suspenseful, intense, and truly haunting book with a fuse long and masterfully laid."

Los Angeles Review of Books

WE SPREAD

Iain Reid

Published by Scribner Canada

New York   London   Toronto   Sydney   New Delhi

SCRIBNER
CANADA

Scribner Canada
An Imprint of Simon & Schuster, Inc.
166 King Street East, Suite 300
Toronto, Ontario M5A 1J3

This Scribner Canada edition September 2022

SCRIBNER CANADA and colophon are trademarks of Simon & Schuster, Inc.

For information about special discounts for bulk purchases, please contact Simon & Schuster Special Sales at 1-800-268-3216 or CustomerService@simonandschuster.ca.

Interior design by Lexy Alemao

Manufactured in the United States of America

10 9 8 7 6 5 4 3 2 1

Library and Archives Canada Cataloguing in Publication

Title: We spread / Iain Reid.
Names: Reid, Iain, 1981– author.
Identifiers: Canadiana (print) 20210392533 | Canadiana (ebook) 20210392568 |
    ISBN 9781982165055 (hardcover) | ISBN 9781982165062 (ebook)
Classification: LCC PS8635.E399 W4 2022 | DDC C813/.6—dc23

ISBN 978-1-9821-6505-5
ISBN 978-1-9821-6506-2 (ebook)

To Eliza

WE SPREAD

Part One

He was an artist. A prolific painter of merit and distinction. He impressed with his boldness and ingenuity. He liked to shock and bewilder. He refined this aesthetic of orderly, exaggerated confusion over many years. He gained admirers, patrons, imitators. "Parrots" is what he called the younger artists he felt were trying to replicate his flair. One reviewer wrote about feeling "emotionally mauled" by his work. All the time I knew him, he never wavered from his claim that his only obsession was producing more work and never burning out or fading away.

He received fan mail at our apartment—cards and letters would arrive from all over the country, even from Europe. Sometimes they would simply be addressed to the Artist, which made him roll his eyes in mock humility. He was discussed and interpreted by students. He would give guest lectures where those in attendance would ask him to clarify and expand on his work and to share any advice he could with aspiring artists. He was not famous the way a musician or actor is. But in a particular niche of surrealist devotees, he was revered and celebrated.

But none of them knew him the way I did. I knew him in the most intimate ways one person can know another. I knew him in a way no one else did, not his fans or friends or family. I knew him, I believe, as he knew himself.

Over our many years together I bore witness to the invisible anatomy that formed his identity. They thought he was immune to trends, to fitting in. He was not. He required a commonwealth of reaction and sought acceptance. He was loud in everything he did.

Some realizations about those closest to us arrive in a flash. Other insights take decades to form. My partner's work conveyed something spiritual, but he was so human after all, mortal, a man who, like so many others, grew less interested, less curious, less attentive over time. It was both endearing and disappointing. He was, I came to see, more than anything, a conformist.

We weren't miserable together. We fought like any couple, especially when we were young. But in later years we would quarrel over nonsense like what temperature to set the thermostat. Some evenings during our first years together, we would drink white wine and speak broken French to each other. Even if we didn't completely understand it, we loved the sound of the language.

As we grew older, we spent more time apart, even when we were both home in the apartment. He despised aging and didn't trust his crumbling body. The love I'd felt for him faded and detached. There was nothing to hold it in place. No more mystery. Nothing to learn. Wonder was replaced with awareness. By the end, it wasn't just familiarity. I had a total and complete understanding of him.

He used to say I was moody and too sympathetic for my own good. He said I avoided confrontation and that he'd spent years trying to make me less anxious, less meek and mild, and that I was always in some kind of inner revolt. He worried about trivialities just as much as I did. The difference was, unlike me, he could hide it.

Before he died, when he was very sick, he told me how frightened he was. He was terrified of becoming obsolete and forgotten. He'd never admitted being scared before that. Never. He said when you're so close to death, when it's right there, the depth of fear is enormous. He didn't want to die. He desperately wanted more time. He said he had so much more he wanted to do. He said he was scared for me, too, scared that I would have to go through the end of life alone.

He was right about that. I am near the end now, and I am alone. Very old and very much alone. I have been both for some time, surrounded by the listless stacks and heavy piles of a life already lived: vinyl records, empty flowerpots, clothing, dishes, photo albums, magazines about art, drawings, letters from friends, the library of paperback books lining my shelves. It's no wonder I'm stuck in the past, thinking about him, our days together, how our relationship started, and how it ended. I feel enveloped by the past. I've lived here in the same apartment for more than fifty years. The man I moved here with, the man I spent more time with over my life than anyone else, would tell me in private moments, right here in the apartment, while lying in our bed, that my being too sensitive would be my demise.

"You were the sensitive one," I say now, to the empty room. "You were the fearful one."

I'm not left with anger or resentment or pity. It's an anticlimax—a mourning for my own naive belief.

I look around my living room.

There are piles of notebooks and sketch pads, drawings and photographs. The first piece of art I ever owned is buried in here somewhere. A gift from my father. It's a tiny framed print of the tree of life that's small enough to fit one hand. I never hung it because I didn't want anyone else to see it.

There are two bookshelves full of paperbacks. I'm losing my attention span; it's hard to read novels now, or books of any kind. I used to read a book or two a week. Literary fiction, historical novels, comedies. I devoured books on science and nature.

There is a box under the coffee table full of small, ceramic sculptures. I made them in my midtwenties. I have all these records, but I don't listen to music anymore.

At one time, it wasn't just stuff. It all meant so much to me. All of it. Marrow that has turned to fat.

My living room chair is the only place I sit. It's where I watch TV. It's where I nap. It's where I eat. I have a bowl of red soup in front of me on my tray, a single lamp lighting the room. I ate the first half of the can for supper last night. I sip the salty broth without pleasure. I don't sleep well at night. My body is tired. My knee aches.

I sit here in my chair from late afternoon until dark, when I realize it must be time for bed. I don't have much of an appetite. I never did, but it has diminished with age. I'm not turned off by food. I understand that it is essential. I mostly sip my soup for its warmth, which is lost by the last few spoonfuls. Consuming greedily, gorging the way some do, was never appealing to me. I couldn't do it. I eat slowly. Hot food always grows cold.

I used to enjoy cooking for myself and for others. I adored watching friends eat the food I'd made them. I'd take pleasure in cleaning the dirty napkins after a meal, relics of shared satisfaction. We'd have large, raucous dinner parties every few weeks. We'd open wine and discuss politics, art, religion, music, film. We'd dance, sing, play games, laugh.

We knew most of our friends from the art world, but we'd also include neighbors from our building, and people we knew from the neighborhood. I'd invite colleagues from work. My day job was a teller at the same bank for more than twenty-five years. The job mostly involved filing deposit slips. The last time I was there, ages ago, I didn't know a single face. I didn't recognize anyone.

I used to make a huge pot of rich bone broth the color of mahogany every Sunday. It became a winter tradition. The apartment would slowly fill up with its nourishing smell, which would stay on our clothes for days. I would roast whole chickens two at a time and make mushroom omelets with an arugula salad dressed with a lemon vinaigrette. My buttermilk biscuits were famous in the building. I'd always make enough to give half of them away.

But my favorite meal was the simplest. A single fried egg, over easy, with a piece of buttered toast to dip in the yolk. I learned to make it when I was around nine or ten. This lunch, with a hot cup of tea, was something that sustained me over and over again. Now the thing I eat most often is soup and dry soda crackers.

I scan the living room again. Everything's so old-fashioned. Even I can see that. Outdated. Worn out. This used to actually be a room for living. Now it's no more than a mangy depository. A shabby and confined storehouse for old newspapers, random trinkets, carpet stains, and me.

I bring a spoonful of soup to my nose and sniff before tasting. I can't smell anything. I fumble the empty spoon onto the floor by my feet. When I bend to pick it up, I feel my chest tighten and I start to cough. Just lightly at first, but it becomes a fit.

When the coughing finally stops, I can feel the tears on my cheeks.

Another long night of tossing and turning in the dark. Nights shouldn't feel as long as days. Nights are meant to go by in the blink of an eye. I'm supposed to wake up feeling rested and refreshed. But I never do.

I have no idea what time it is. My covers are up to my chin, but I still feel a chill. My bedroom, like the living room, is cramped and cluttered. I don't have the energy to get rid of anything. I shift my position, moving over to the other side of the mattress. Despite being tired, I can't fall asleep.

Just as I feel myself drifting off, I hear a voice, high-pitched, from the other side of the wall.

"Stop," I hear. "Listen."

I didn't realize I had any neighbors right next door, on the other side of the wall. I thought the tenant there had left weeks ago. She's loud and firm without yelling. She sounds serious. It's too muffled to make out what else she's saying. I hear a chair fall over, or a door close.

I roll onto my stomach, trying desperately to fall sleep, using my thin pillow to muffle the noise.

'm going through my morning routine in the bathroom the same way I do every morning, brushing my teeth, washing my face. I splash a handful of warm water onto my cheeks. I used to have smooth skin; strangers would tell me I looked young for my age. My white hair is thinning and flat. I stopped coloring it a few years ago. I've always been short, lean, but I've lost weight. I know without stepping on a scale. I'm scrawny now, withered. I'm parched and shrunken like dried fruit. I've never moved gracefully, but my arthritic knee has made me slower and even more inelegant. It aches.

Once dressed, I time myself using the clock hanging on the wall, and it takes nine minutes for me to get ready, bundling up in my jacket, boots, gloves, scarf, hat. Nine full minutes. I imagine it's as time-consuming as it would be preparing a toddler. Almost ten minutes just to leave my apartment in winter. All this to get a few groceries.

I descend in the elevator, exit my building, and walk along the slushy sidewalk, wheeling a small cart behind me. I walk slowly, carefully, past an office building's large ground-floor window. I would pass this building on my way to the bank each day. I pause when I see my full reflection in the glass. My hunch has worsened. When did I stop taking care of myself?

Perhaps this physical decline was inevitable. It's what he dreaded most: seeing a depleted shape looking back in the mirror, the feeling that he'd lost his chance to create. Could he have done anything to stop it? Could I? To reverse it? The finish line always, eventually, arrives. It has to.

That's life. It's the tragedy of life: the end comes for us all. People on the sidewalk pass me by, stepping around me, without eye contact or acknowledgment.

Back home, back on the third floor, I sit inside door 3B to remove my boots. I don't have the pep to remove my coat or unpack the cart of groceries. My body might be giving up on me, but my mind has been less depleted by age. I can still think. I know what day of the week it is, the season. I can converse with strangers while standing in line at the store if need be. I'm grateful for the compromise. That's what has always worried me most. Cognitive decline. Fading memories. Lost days. An uncertain present.

I walk over to the bookshelf, looking for a specific book. When I find it, I remove it from the shelf and take it over to my chair. *Surrealism* by Herbert Read. I flip to a page marked with a napkin. I read aloud a sentence at random.

" 'The Surrealist movement was a revolution directed at every sphere of life, encompassing politics and poetry as well as art, its purpose the liberation of resources of the subconscious mind. . . .' "

Art and surrealism encompassed my life, too. More than anything else. I loved this book when I bought it.

I was so excited to get home and read it. The ideas in it felt so alive to me, connected to what I aspired to be. It felt personally linked to me by the emotion it aroused within me. I remember I'd been working on a self-portrait when I bought it. I don't know what ever happened to that painting. I'm sure it's still here somewhere among a pile of others.

I can remember with such specificity the feelings I had then, a private, internal frenzy of potential. Where is that now? Frames of mind aren't built to last. They aren't dependable. Even the sturdiest eventually dissolve and disappear.

I set the book down on the side table and finally remove my hat and unzip my heavy coat. I lean over and write three names on the flattened, unused napkin from my lunch.

Arshile Gorky, Meret Oppenheim, Leonora Carrington.

There was a time when seeing the names of these artists thrilled me. It didn't even have to be their work, just seeing their names. I read the names over a few times and then set the napkin down atop a short pile of other handwritten notes.

There are several of these piles all around the apartment. Sometimes I find my notes in the creases of the chair or in the pockets of my sweaters. The notes started as mundane memos to myself, about recipes, or grocery lists. But they've become more urgent over the months. My memory is strong. I'm writing these notes preemptively. I'm writing them because I know I'm very old and soon I'll forget. I'll forgot all these things that excite me, thrill me. All the things I adore. I'll forget the feelings I felt. Then it will be too late to try to remember.

I remove two notes that I find in the pocket of my cardigan hanging over the back of my chair.

There's more bread in the freezer.

You always loved to dance.

A muted thump from next door wakes me. Then, a cough. A voice. A woman's. Displeased but assertive. She must live next door. The apartment beside me. I thought it was empty. I thought the last tenants moved out. My mouth is dry, and I'm thirsty. It's still dark now, and I wonder how much longer until morning.

Most nights my sleep feels feeble and flimsy but full of troubled dreams. I have a reoccurring dream of being in the park near my apartment. I don't go there much anymore, but I used to walk there almost every morning before work. I loved seeing the huge, old trees, how the first light from the rising sun made the grass look like a moving painting. I would sit on a bench and feel the breeze on my face. But I had to get there at the right time or I'd miss it. It would never last long. That's what made it special.

In the dream, I'm trying to get there, to the park, to the bench, but people keep stopping me on the way. It's frustrating and frantic. It's getting lighter and brighter, and I know I'm not going to make it. I wake up, fall asleep, wake up, fall asleep in an endless cycle until my room is filled with daylight. The dreams come and go. I never look at my clock until I'm up and out of bed.

Once, he told me I should try painting a landscape, as an exercise. He said portraits are so specific and small. He said I should expand my areas of interest, challenge myself, acknowledge a grander scale. So I painted some of the trees from the park to appease him.

He saw the first piece when I was halfway through it. He studied it, taking his glasses down from the top of his head, and said: "I don't see trees, Penny. Not at all. This is not an insult. I'm just encouraging you to try painting more sincerely. To paint what you actually see."

I never did finish that painting.

I roll over and flip on the soft bedside lamp. I run my hand along my forearm. There's a bruise there, and the spot is sensitive to the touch. I don't think I had this bruise when I went to bed, so how did I get it?

"We can't stop it now," the voice says from the other side of the wall.

"I know that," a deeper voice replies.

I stop rubbing my arm. I'm listening. I've been hearing these voices from next door more and more, usually at night. They're only sounds, disembodied tones, but they are real. Voices aren't sounds like the cars and buses and sirens from outside. These ones have a distinctive impact on me. The sounds of humans.

I hear footsteps and a door slam shut. What time is it? I lie in the dark, eyes wide open, awake.

"How do you feel?"

I can't make out the exact response. I've missed it.

"No! You can't say anything. Especially not to her."

Another muffled reply.

"You're not listening!"

Then, silence. I lean over, switch on the lamp, and scrawl a note to myself.

Ask Mike about the voices next door.

I get up.

My slippers make it harder to walk. They're heavy and stick on the carpet. But without them, my little feet are too cold. During the days, I sit more than I walk anyway. I sit and watch the TV. I sit and I eat. I sit and look at my changed hands, the dark spots and protruding veins, how bony and curved my fingers have become. They look more like knotted twigs than usable human fingers, more like bark than skin.

I wish I had done more. There's not enough time for me now. I had years and years' worth of time. It went so fast. It went too fast.

I shuffle to the washroom and then crawl back into bed. I've never removed the empty litter box from under the window, even though there's no need for it now. When did the cat die? Gorky loved to cuddle, especially in the morning. It seems a long time ago now.

Every now and then, I still hear her, Gorky, softly mewing from one of the rooms. It takes me a moment to realize it's only an illusion, an auditory figment born from loneliness and memory.

Above the litter box two oil paintings hang on the bedroom wall. Massive landscapes. Two of his earliest ones that, for sentimental reasons, he said he could never sell. They're so big, heavy, like all his work. Does scale on its own show aspiration? Does dimension relate to achievement? I don't like these paintings of his. I avoid them. I never told him the truth of what I thought. He was fond of them. I would take them down if I could reach them and was strong enough. They're too heavy for me to move. They always were.

There are other canvases, too, smaller paintings of mine, leaning backward against the wall in the corner of the room. We never hung any of my portraits. I didn't want to. I didn't feel the need to display them that way, and I never felt like they were finished. I always wanted the chance to keep working on them, tinkering, revising, revisiting. I was only confident in the excitement I felt and in my dedication to the work itself. Not in the end result. I didn't believe I could produce anything to affect or inspire others.

"How can you be an artist if you never let people see any of your pictures?" he asked me. "You need the viewer as much as they need you. Otherwise, it's not art you're making."

I did have that far-off ambition hidden away somewhere, I suppose, that there was a chance I might produce something that another person might respond to. But I never told him that. I never told anyone. Even alone now, it makes me ashamed to think I'd hoped it might happen.

The week after he died, I took out my box of my ceramic sculptures. I removed one and set it on my beside. It's still there. It was the first sculpture I ever made. Its amateurishness had always embarrassed me. The clay figurine is a person with their head tilted to one side.

I pick it up, exam it, rubbing my thumb over it. I never would have admitted to anyone, but I'd felt such thrill making it.

I'm starting to lose the intimacy of my memories. Most of my memories have stopped feeling like my own. I don't believe them wholeheartedly the way I used to, and they don't carry the same heft they once did.

It's sad. It's sad how I live. Isn't clarity supposed to come with age and experience? If I had more time, I could make changes. I could learn more. I could work more, paint more. I could be better than I am. That's what I regret most. Knowing I could have been a better, more accomplished painter, but now it's too late. It all comes down to not having enough time. I wish I could go back.

I turn the lamp off. Unable to fall asleep, I start quietly humming to myself, a lullaby.

I feel like I've barely slept. My lips are cracked. I touch them with my finger as I walk into the living room. I've left the TV on from the night before. It's muted. I sit and turn up the volume. It's loud. I squint at the screen. It's a nature show about insects and other small creatures.

"Little, old honeybees. We take them for granted, but they're actually smart enough to engage in mathematics," the announcer says in a deep, soothing voice.

I watch as a tiny bee extracts pollen from a red flower. I stand up, walk back to my bedroom, and rummage around in my closet until I find what I'm looking for: an old set of oil paints. I can still hear the TV from in here.

"Bees understand math and can even solve simple puzzles based on elementary arithmetic. . . ."

I never understood math. It's just not the way my brain works. It's a whole world I could never inhabit.

The case is dented and dusty. I hold the set in my hand for a moment, wondering how long I've had it. I sit down and open one of the canisters. The paint has dried and is unusable. I haven't painted in years. I lean over and pick up one my paintings in the corner, leaning against the wall.

It's an unfinished portrait, one of the last I worked on. I don't recognize the subject. Who is this person? Someone I must have been close with. A childhood friend? I don't feel any connection to this piece anymore. Nothing.

How can that be?

Another day come and gone. Another night to endure in my bed. A soft, almost imperceptible knock on my wall. Just one. It's a delicate knock, but it startles me. How many days has it been since I've been hearing these sounds? Two? Three? A week?

In the darkness, the knock somehow seems directed at me, as if one of the people next door, I think the man, is trying to tell me something, warn me of something. I lean over and knock back, very lightly. I hear nothing. I do it again, louder, with more force. I wait, hoping to hear a response, when a dry spot in my throat causes me to cough. It tickles, and despite my urge to remain silent, it only gets worse.

I put on my slippers and barely reach the kitchen when I'm in the throes of a full coughing fit. I'm holding on to the counter, keeled over. When the hacking finally subsides, I spit into the sink. A thread of saliva dangles from my bottom lip.

There's a single potato sitting by the sink. I've had it there for weeks, maybe months. I took it out to bake. It's sprouting now.

There's life locked in that simple, dormant potato. That little sprout will keep growing, and start moving toward the window and the light, the longer it grows.

Just this morning, as I made my tea, I listened to an interview on the radio with a professor, a plant biologist. It made me think of my father. He had such a fascination with nature and biology. As a child, he would tell me tidbits about trees and plants, how amazing they are, how durable and sturdy. I stood beside the radio and turned it up, thinking about Dad.

She talked about an experiment with two plants growing together and how it was possible for the cells of the individual plants to end up gathering meaningful amounts of DNA from the other. It was fascinating. I listened, transfixed. She went on to explain how horizontal transfers of genes were not abnormal in bacteria, fungi, and even plants. It happens when one organism moves genetic material to another that isn't its own offspring.

A plant pursues life at all costs. I decide I should jot down her words.

Horizontal transfers of genes.

Pursuit of life at all costs.

Just as I'm putting down my pencil, the phone on the wall starts ringing, which startles me. It rarely rings anymore and never this late. My phone is near a window, and by the time I get there, it has stopped ringing. I stand looking out at the dark street. Two people walk by with a dog; cars pass.

Just before turning back, I notice a figure across the street. A person in a hat and jacket. Their face is obscured. Unlike the other pedestrians, and the cars driving by, the figure is completely still.

I step closer to the window.

The figure is not moving at all. How can a person stand like that, so perfectly inert, so fixated?

They appear to be staring up toward my window. At me. I can't see their face. There's a calmness to the stance. They are untroubled. So why does it make me uncomfortable? Why does it frighten me? I feel observed, violated.

I lean away from the window, hiding. I wait as a couple of sets of headlights move along the wall as cars drive by. I build up my courage to lean back over to the window.

But when I do, the figure on the street is gone.

'm standing in my baggy cardigan with the sleeves rolled up, hunching over one of my unfinished portraits. I know it's my work. I'm certain of it. But I feel no bond to it, no affiliation. I stare at it, feeling nothing. A loud, abrupt knock on the door startles me.

I walk to the front entrance and wait for another knock before I put my eye to the peephole: a bald man dressed in a blue uniform, holding a tool bag at his side.

"Yes?" I say, through the locked door.

"Here for the maintenance check."

"I didn't ask for anyone to come."

I see him roll his eyes.

"It's been scheduled for weeks," he says.

I don't know what else to do, so I unlock the dead bolt, the chain, and let him in. He sets his leather kit down and peers around the room.

"It's a routine upgrade. We're doing it in all the units."

"Mike should tell me these things," I say. "I should be warned in advance."

"He was supposed to let everyone know."

"Well, he didn't!" I snap.

He starts taking out some tools.

"Do you have an outlet in your room?"

"By the bed," I say. "And one in the closet. But please don't touch anything in there."

"I won't," he says. "I'll be back."

He leaves me standing in the living room. I move closer to the wall and listen to this stranger working in my bedroom. I hear a drill and some pounding. When he returns, he starts to gather his equipment.

"I see you still have radiant heat," he says. "Are they working okay? Feels a bit cold in here."

"The radiators?"

"Yeah."

"They're working. Was that you?" I ask. "Last night. Were you out on the street?"

He stops what he's doing and looks at me.

"The street?"

"Was that you, out there . . . watching me?"

"I'm just here to change your outlets," he says. "I don't want any trouble."

"Have you been there yet?" I ask, pointing to the wall that separates my apartment from the next one over.

"I did that unit before yours."

"Did you talk to them?"

"Who?"

"The tenants."

"No one's living there. It's vacant. Listen, I still have more units to get through."

I feel my face flush.

"Are you okay? Is someone checking in on you from time to time?"

I don't immediately reply.

"I'm . . . fine," I say.

"Okay. Take care of yourself."

After he leaves, I follow his path to the door and open it, just enough to see through. I watch him walk all the way down the hall. He doesn't stop at any of the other doors. He gets to the end of the hall, waits for the elevator, and leaves without looking back.

I realize I never asked him for identification. That's what I'm supposed to do if an uninvited guest shows up. I kneel on the floor of my bedroom, examining one of the newly installed outlets. It looks the same as before. There's no obvious difference. Did he even replace anything?

If he didn't replace the outlet, why was he in my apartment? What was he doing in my room?

'm down on the floor with a roll of Scotch tape; the only sticky thing I could find. I can feel my forehead perspiring. I put a piece of tape over the new outlet. And then another. I put enough tape to completely cover it. The outlets are all taped now, all of them that are not in use.

I get up and walk into the kitchen. I'm not hungry, but I don't think I've eaten yet today. I find my last can of red soup, which I manage to open without trouble and pour into a pot on the stove. I fill the empty can with water and stir it into the mixture. As I wait for the soup to heat, the single kitchen light bulb starts to flicker and then burns out.

I hadn't noticed it's grown dark outside. I look up at the bulb. I push a chair underneath the light. I shouldn't do this. I know I shouldn't. I should wait and get Mike to do it.

I climb up onto the chair, slowly, and with great effort bring a foot up onto the back of the chair. I'm reaching my hand toward the light, my arm in front of my face. It doesn't look like my own arm, but someone else's. I'm so close. As I'm about to touch it. I lose my balance and fall onto the floor, hitting my forehead on the counter.

The wind is knocked out of me. I can't get a breath.

I try to roll over. A sharp pain in my forehead. I lie on the floor. I hear the soup bubbling over on the stove, hissing.

It takes a minute to realize I'm still on the kitchen floor. I don't know how long I've been down here. My side is sore from the hard ground. I must have been unconscious. For how long? I can move my arms and legs, but I can't seem to get up.

I bring my hand to my head. My forehead is cut and bleeding from a single gash. I close my eyes, resting my head on my hands, giving in to the pain.

When I wake again, I don't know how long I've been out. Hours?

My head throbs. I bring my hand to my head and feel that the blood has dried. The kitchen is dark. It must be the middle of the night. I can smell burnt soup. I didn't turn off the stove. I look around. I'm still alone, but then I see . . . movement.

My bedroom is across from the kitchen, and the door is closed. I think I see a subtle shift through the crack at the bottom of my door, from inside my room. I wait. I definitely see a change in the light, as if someone is walking inside my room.

I try to get up again, but I can't. I flop on to my chest. I close my eyes as tight as I can. I should call for help. I should yell out to the person in my room.

But I'm too scared. Who is it, and why are they here? I don't think they're here to help me. If they were, wouldn't they have noticed me by now? I'm trying not to make any noise that could attract attention. I start to drag myself out of the kitchen into the hall. I need to get away from whoever is in my room.

I hear the creaking of a door opening, my bedroom door, and then a soft footstep. A high heel, it sounds like. And then another step, coming toward me.

I don't look back. I continue crawling until I'm in between the kitchen and living room. I want to keep going, to crawl my way to safety, but I can't. The pain is too severe. I'm exhausted. I lie on my chest and close my eyes.

When I open my eyes, I see the hazy outline of a man hover- ing over me. There's daylight in the room. I know him. My landlord, Mike. Unshaven, in a white T-shirt, like always. Was it him in my room? When was that? He's leaning over me, speaking, but his words sound muffled and far away.

"Penny . . . Hey, Penny? You hear me?"

He puts his hand on my shoulder.

"Goddammit, Penny. Don't do this to me."

I open my eyes wider and try to roll onto my side.

"Good," he says. "That's good. You're okay. Come on. Let's get you up."

Part Two

'm buckled in to Mike's foul-smelling car, trying not to move or touch anything. We're snaking our way in and out of several lanes of traffic, starting, stopping. The lurching motion is making me queasy. There are what look like grease stains on the edge of my seat. The snow from my boots has melted onto the floor mat.

I look out at the busy street, the city where I've always lived, my whole life. I bring a hand to my forehead and touch the scab from my fall. It's still tender.

I've been in my apartment for decades, and it only took a matter of days to get rid of me. Days. Mike said most of my stuff was put in storage. He wanted me to stay in bed the whole time, resting after the fall, so he could sort through my things and load it all more efficiently. He hired movers to help. In between troubled sleeps, I could hear it all happening, but I was powerless to stop it. Garbage bags and boxes being filled, talking, laughing, tape being cut, vacuuming, dishes being stacked.

IAIN REID

At one point, two strangers came in to look at the wound on my head. One of them said it looked better and removed the bandage.

The few things deemed essential were packed up this morning. I haven't had a bath since my fall.

"What's going on?" I say. "Where are we going?"

"Come on, Penny. We've already gone over this. It's time."

"What are you talking about?"

"You know you can't stay there alone forever," he says. "It's too dangerous for you to be alone."

"I'm fine," I say. "I like being alone."

"You're not fine," he says. "If I hadn't found you, you could have . . ."

With one hand, he reaches for a folder full of papers that's sitting on the armrest between us. He looks from the road down to the folder and back to the road again. He slips a piece of paper from the folder and sets it on my lap. It's a photo of an old house surrounded by trees.

"You're lucky. Most people in your situation don't have options. He gave me all the paperwork before he died. It's lucky he prepared for this. You both did."

"What do you mean?"

"That you planned where you'd go. He said you picked this place because of all the nature. He wanted you to stay in the apartment for as long as possible, but when it was too much—"

"Too much?"

"When it was too much for you to cope with on your own, that's when I was to take you here. Don't you remember? The two of you decided this years ago."

"Where?" I ask, looking at the photo again. I don't recognize it. I don't remember deciding anything. "A house? An old-age home? I don't need that. I'm not helpless. I'm not sick."

"It's not an old-age home. It's a long-term-care residence. It's supposed to be really nice. Very small. Quiet. They'll look after you."

"He never said anything to me about this. Not a word. I would remember if he had. Neither did you. Why didn't you tell me sooner? You should have warned me. I don't want to leave the apartment. It's my home. Why didn't he tell me about this?"

"He told me this was your choice, Penny."

I feel a sharp pain where my head had hit the counter.

"It's actually very sweet, and if you hadn't planned it and made a deposit, you'd be in trouble now. You'd probably be on a waiting list somewhere."

"I don't want to be taken care of. I want to be left alone. You should have told me, given me some time to prepare."

"Penny, I did. I have. I've mentioned it a few times."

I turn away.

In the side mirror I peer into the back seat. Two bags, several boxes, my canvases: the essentials. Years and years, all boiled down to that. I feel hot. I try to lower the window, but the button won't work. I look to my left, at Mike's profile, but he won't make eye contact. He stares at the road, straight ahead.

After leaving the city, I let my head fall against the window in silent protest, watching as the eight-lane highway turns to four, then just a two-lane road. Out here the terrain is more hilly, mountainous. Tall trees line either side of the road. Hills and sky and clouds. It's all the trees I notice the most. There are so many. They're different from the ones in the park near my apartment. Such tall trees here. Trees that are much older than me. I'd have to cut into them and count the rings to confirm how old they are.

I don't know how long the silence lasts between us, but eventually, his phone interrupts the quiet with directions: "Your destination is on the right."

We pull in and stop at the end of the lane. It doesn't look like a destination to me. It looks like a dirt alley leading into a dense forest. Mike lowers his window. The first thing I hear is the soft whistle of an unrecognizable songbird, and a natural silence that I don't think I've ever experienced in the city, not even in a park.

Mike puts the car in gear and continues onto the lane. More trees on either side. There are trees everywhere. The driveway leads to a stone house up ahead. It's big, older than it looked in the photo, but plain, unspectacular, with thick hedges around one side. There's a weathered green sign out front that I can't read from here.

Mike pulls into a parking spot and turns off the car.

"Come on," he says.

I don't want to get out of the car. I want to go back to the city, to my apartment. I don't even care about my bags. He can throw them out if he wants. I want to sit in my chair. I want to lie in the same slumping bed that I know. I rub a hand over my bad knee. My head throbs.

He comes around to my door, helps me up, and holds my arm as we walk toward the front door. I straighten my shoulders as best I can. The path to the door is uneven, and I have to watch my feet so as not to trip. We're close enough now that I can read the green sign:

SIX CEDARS RESIDENCE

My palms are sweaty. There's a click as the door unlocks. Mike opens it and looks back at me. I hesitate.

"Here we are," he says.

Mike helps me through the door into a foyer. I step from the stone path onto hardwood floor. It's newer inside than it looked from the outside. There's a long coffee table with a bouquet of fresh roses sitting on it and two leather chairs. Mike takes a step closer.

I hear music: the faint sound of a violin.

"Hello?" Mike calls out.

He leans down and raps his knuckles firmly on the top of the table.

I'm trying to take it all in, process this place, when I hear high heels walking down a wooden staircase to the left of the door. A woman in a red dress appears. She's tall, lean. Her long hair is brushed back neatly off her face. I would guess she's about the same age as Mike, maybe fifty? Or maybe she's closer to sixty. It's hard to say.

She stops in front me, grinning. "You must be Penny," she says.

She's beautiful. Her voice is warm, sincere, welcoming. She reaches her hand out toward me. I instinctively take hold of it. Her nails are perfectly manicured, painted the same color as her lipstick and dress.

"It's so nice to meet you," she says.

We shake hands, and for a moment I'm not sure what I should do or say.

"I'm Shelley," the woman says. "We've been waiting for you."

Mike drops the bag he's carrying. "There's more stuff in the car," he says.

The tall woman, Shelley, looks at him. "Mike, right? Thank you so much for arranging everything."

A large cat is circling Mike's feet. He shoos it away.

"I sent you all the paperwork. We're good, right?"

"Yes, yes, everything's all set."

"Is there anything else you're going to need from me?"

"No, we'll be just fine."

As she says this, a young man appears, walking silently down the same staircase she came down. He's skinny, almost gaunt, shorter than her, and dressed in a white top and bottoms like a hospital worker.

"Jack will get the rest of her things from the car," she says.

With a subtle nod, Jack enters a code on a keypad by the door and heads out to the car, leaving the door propped open behind him. Mike lowers his voice, speaking more to the woman, but I can hear him.

"I feel bad about her fall, but I'm not responsible for watching her twenty-four/seven. I got a lot going on there. The plan was to bring her here when it was too much. That's what I've done. I'm just glad nothing worse happened."

The woman smiles again.

"You did the right thing," she says. "She's in the best spot for her now. You're welcome to visit as often as you'd like."

Shelley, still smiling, steps forward, and shakes Mike's hand. Her hands are elegant, strong-looking. They're the hands of a much younger woman than me. They're lovely. I can't help but stare at them. Mike turns back to me from the open doorway.

"Okay. See you later, then, Penny."

"Where are you going?" I ask.

"I have to go back to work. You get to stay here."

"Why are you doing this?"

He doesn't respond, and I can sense his relief of being rid of one nuisance.

Shelley waits until Mike's back inside his car and the engine is going before she turns to look down at me, offering an arm.

"Let's go, my dear," she says. "I'll show you to your room."

Shelley leads me down the narrow hardwood hallway. The violin moans, slightly louder than it was from the foyer.

"That's Pete," she says. "You'll get to meet him. He's been here the longest. Doesn't talk much anymore, but still loves to play."

We pass a large window. I step toward it.

All I can see are trees and sky. Trees as far as the eye can see. The bare branches sway gently in the wind as if waving.

"Beautiful, isn't it?" she says. "I've always loved nature. It's so peaceful here in the forest."

She takes a step closer.

"Because of the surrounding terrain," she continues, "the hills and steep bluffs, we don't permit the residents to go outside unaccompanied. It's too dangerous. But the views from inside are spectacular."

We continue past a cozy sitting area with a bench and two chairs neatly arranged with plush pillows.

"You have access to the whole house, Penny. There's a common room, our own little hair salon, and we serve all our meals in the house's original dining room. We renovated it completely, but it was built in 1843."

We walk slowly, carefully, my hand on her arm for support.

"You'll feel at home in no time. I promise," she says.

A painting hanging on the wall catches my eye. I stop to look at it. I know it. I recognize it.

"We have lots of art around," she says. "I figured you'd appreciate that."

A still life, a table full of food, oysters, half-peeled lemons, grapes. "De Heem," I say.

"You know it?" Shelley says. "I guess I shouldn't be surprised. It's so nice for us to have an artist living here now."

I look up at her. She knows that I paint?

"Don't get too excited," she says. "It's just a print. Not the real thing."

"This feels rushed. I wasn't expecting to be here," I say. "I have my own apartment. I'd like to go home."

"It's going to be an adjustment for you. But you'll get to know us. And to be honest, I know it sounds funny, but I feel like I already know you."

"You do?"

"Yes, we have a lot of details in our file, and I've been looking forward to meeting you and getting you settled. It's so nice to finally have you here."

I remember now what Mike said. That we planned for this day, that he gave a deposit for me to have a spot here. That we picked it because it was in a quiet spot, outside the city, in nature. I wonder, before he died, did he actually send her information about me, about my life? I definitely didn't. Or did Mike? What is it she thinks she knows about me? We continue walking until we reach a red door.

"And here we are."

She steps in first, but I hesitate on the threshold.

"It's okay," she says. "Take your time, Penny."

I step into the room. It's clean, bright. It's warm. The large bed must be a queen. It has a thick duvet and makes me appreciate how modest my double bed was, the bed I shared with him for so long and later had all to myself. There's a recliner chair in a corner, a lamp, a dresser, and a desk. There's a grand window on the far wall facing out to the endless forest.

There's no clutter. No dust. No trinkets. Every surface is polished. It's nothing like my apartment. In fact, it's the opposite.

"Nice, isn't it?"

She's right. It is nice. I can almost feel a weight lifted off my shoulders, not having to think about objects. No debris. All that stuff comes with obligation and duty. It hits me that I won't be the responsible one here. No upkeep or cleaning. No laundry. No shopping. No bills or light bulbs to change. No decision-making.

Shelley leads me to the chair, easing me down. It's as if she thinks I can't walk on my own, that I'm so delicate I might fall again. I might have a bad knee and sore head, but I don't need this kind of attention. I'm not decrepit.

This chair is nothing like my old one. It must be brand-new. I might be the first person to ever sit in it. I sink into it. I feel like I'm being hugged. The skinny fellow in white, Jack, enters the room, carrying a box of my things.

I watch as he starts unpacking some clothes, putting them into the dresser and closet. How did they get packed? Was it Mike? I didn't do that. I don't remember packing anything. But my clothes are here. I look around the room again. I've never lived anywhere this nice before. Not in my whole life.

Jack leaves, and again, I'm alone with her.

"I didn't ask for this," I say. "I can look after myself."

"I know," she says.

"Then why am I here?"

"You picked us, Penny. With your husband," she says.

"We were never married."

"You lived with a man."

"I did, yes, for many years."

"It was his last gift to you. He was in contact with us and arranged it all. He wanted to make sure you'd have nothing to worry about. The two of you had foresight that many don't have."

"Did he pay for all this?"

"You don't have to worry about that. Six Cedars isn't one of those places that's looking to turn a big profit. We do this because we love taking caring of our elders. It's a privilege."

"Why didn't Mike remind me?"

"Mike's been keeping us up to date on how you've been doing."

"Why would we pick here? Why not somewhere closer to the city?"

"Because we're a small and peaceful facility. You love nature, don't you?"

"I do. I used to walk to the park near my apartment."

"Then it was a good choice. You'll love it here. I live here, too, right upstairs. So does Jack. We're all here together."

Jack walks back in with two of my bags.

"Thanks, Jack," she says to him. "I'm going to get the others together for the meeting, if you can finish here with Penny."

He nods as Shelley walks out.

"See you soon, Penny," she says.

I watch him lug in more stuff, arms full, including the box of my canvases. He puts them in my closet. He takes a moment to look at some of the paintings, pausing on a couple in particular.

"These are really good. It's nice to see some of your work," he says. "If you need anything at all let me know."

I'm in a new room with new furniture and new smells with a young man I've never met until ten minutes ago. What am I supposed to do? What am I supposed to say?

"I don't remember picking this place," I say.

Jack stops when I speak.

"That's okay," he says. "We're glad you're here."

"I haven't been sleeping well," I say. "Not for a long time."

"You'll sleep well here," he says. "I think you'll sleep very well. Everyone does. Shelley wants everything as comfortable as possible."

His voice is thin, reedy, like his body.

"Those paintings that you were looking at. They aren't finished," I say.

We hear a burst of laughter coming from somewhere. It's uproarious—a high-pitched shriek, followed by clapping and cheering.

"Sounds like the others are ready to meet you," he says.

Jack helps me along, holding my arm, the way Shelley did. We've only just met, but I'm comfortable walking with him like this. I feel safe. Secure. I feel my head swiveling, turning back and forth, up and down, as I try to take it all in: the floor, walls, the ceiling, the windows, the furniture.

The interior of this house is deceptive. It doesn't make sense. From the outside, it looked old, grand, palatial, intimidating. But now, inside, walking along the hall, it feels intimate, charming, cozy.

"Who is the tall woman?" I ask.

"Shelley?"

"Yes. Is she the landlord?"

When he smiles, I see that he is missing one tooth at the side near the back.

"She's the manager. It's an old family house, but she converted it into Six Cedars. It's her life's work. She's really smart and passionate about elder care. She actually has a degree in some kind of organic chemistry or biology. She has a lot of theories about long-term care, about living the best life for as long as possible. We're in good hands."

We arrive at the entrance of a bright, spacious sitting room. When I see the chairs and other people, I freeze. I've never liked public speaking. I never liked introducing myself, talking about myself, explaining who I am to others.

"Come on," he says. He leans closer and whispers. "They're excited to meet you."

Three people, all old, like me, sitting in a spaced semicircle around Shelley. There's one empty chair waiting for me. Shelley waves me over.

"Penny, you're just in time. Please come in, come in."

I clutch Jack's arm as he takes me to the circle. I'm glad he's with me.

Only one of the other residents, a woman with a short bob haircut, the same style I used to have when I was in my early twenties, turns toward me. The others don't move. I'm relieved. I don't want attention or fuss. I hate the spotlight.

The short-haired woman brings one hand in the shape of an O up to her eye as if she's looking through a telescope. She waves at me with the other.

Even though I'm worried about what's next, what it will be like here, what will be expected of me, it is calming to see others who look like me, who are my age, my contemporaries.

Jack leads me over to the only free chair in the circle and eases me down.

"Thanks," Shelley says to him.

He nods and walks out of the room.

I look at the other old faces around me. Along with the short-haired woman, there are two others, both men—a chubby, bald one and a dashing gentleman in a tie and tweed jacket. His white hair is perfectly combed. Though he's sitting, I can tell he is tall. He has a long, lined, hangdog face.

"I want you all to meet Penny."

I wave at no one in particular.

"Bonjour, madame," the short-haired woman says. "So nice to see you, to meet you. You're lovely. Very pretty. How old are you? You don't have to answer that. I know it's a rude question. It's unfair to ask that so soon. Ignore it; ignore me if you want. You're one of us now. That's the important thing. One of us."

Neither of the men says anything, perhaps because they don't want to compete with the talkative one, but the white-haired man in the tie nods and smiles.

"Ruth here is our language expert," Shelley says. "She can speak French, Latin, and a few other languages, too."

"Some Greek," adds Ruth. "Mostly French, though. There's so much to learn with each language. They're all so interesting. Languages are dying out around the world, and it's tragic. But there's something about French."

"Language is good for the brain," says Shelley. "And it's good to talk."

"Like eating fish," says Ruth, touching her temple. "Good for our brains." She looks at me. "Penny. Pennies, Pennies from heaven. We've been waiting for you."

"And that's Hilbert," says Shelley, interrupting and pointing at the man with the tie. "And he's Pete."

The bald man. Some drool escapes from the side of his mouth. Pete looks like he's the oldest of all of us. By several years. He doesn't even make eye contact with me, but Hilbert smiles again, nods, which relaxes me.

"We like to meet like this most days, Penny, to talk, check in."

"We love talking," says Ruth.

"Some of us more than others," says Shelley, raising her eyebrows. "It's a chance to touch base, share, sing a song, laugh, tell a story, discuss something new."

"We can tell any kind of story we want," says Ruth.

"That's mostly true, Ruth," says Shelley. "Before you arrived, Penny, Hilbert was telling us about—"

"Approximating by fractions," Hilbert says.

His voice is calm, deep, steady. I like the sound of it.

"Sometimes we'd rather just be sleeping," says Ruth.

"Pete gives the best violin concerts," says Shelley.

"Does no one care about the fractions?" says Hilbert. "It's one number, but it represents a part of the whole. I'm a fraction. Penny, you are, too."

Shelley laughs but stays still. Her posture is stiff. She doesn't smooth out her dress or pick at her nails. She holds her hands in front of her.

"We don't want to get overly technical, Hilbert," Shelley says, looking at him.

"Fractions and fragments are wonderful," says Ruth. "Talking is wonderful. Being together is wonderful."

"That's right. Chatting can be therapeutic," says Shelley. "Tell us: Have you always lived in the city, Penny?"

"My whole life, yes."

Until today, I think. Until right now.

"It's exciting to think that all this will be a new experience for you."

"An adventure!" says Ruth.

The word fills me with anxiety. I don't want to be on an adventure. Not at all. I want to be home. I want to be having a nap. These people all know each other, are all used to living side by side, but they don't know me. I don't know them.

They're all strangers.

I look back to the door and see the cat walk by. Its coloring is the same as Gorky's, the cat I had long ago, a fluffy piece of butterscotch candy with a tail.

"Not just living outside of the hustle and bustle," says Shelley, "but that we're here to look after you, take care of you. That will be new for you, too, I think. To be spoiled and pampered. You're going to fit right in."

Ruth is about to speak, but then she covers her mouth. It's as though she realizes she's not supposed to say what she was about to.

"And since all our rooms are now filled, and we're operating at capacity, I want to tell you all that we've been planning to throw a little party."

All the rooms are filled? There are only four of us. Six if counting Shelley and Jack. I don't think I've ever heard of a long-term-care facility with only four residents. Were they holding my room for me?

"There are only six of us in the whole residence?" I blurt out.

All eyes on me again. I shouldn't have said anything.

"We are, each of us, one-sixth. A fraction of the whole," says Hilbert. "0.16666666 . . ."

"I'm only one," I say.

"I like a modest scale. My vision has always been to keep this place small, intimate, where we all really get to know one another," says Shelley. "The big care facilities are too impersonal and feel like run-down hospitals. They smell bad. We were delighted to wait for you, Penny. A place this size is much easier to maintain in the way I deem important, in a human way. No one can fall through the cracks. We're a community."

"So . . . a . . . party, you say?" asks Hilbert skeptically.

"Sounds fun!" says Ruth, applauding. "En français: une fête!"

"Yes, something to look forward to," says Shelley.

"Très bien."

Hilbert makes eye contact, leans toward me. "Do you enjoy parties?"

"I used to," I say. "But it's been a while since I've been to one. A long while."

Jack appears at the door, poking his head around the corner.

"Dinner's ready," he says.

"Sounds good," says Shelley. "Okay, everyone. Time to eat."

We file out, one at a time, back into the narrow hall, to the dining room, which isn't as big as the common room. It's all happening too fast. I was just starting to settle in the chair, to feel slightly at ease, and now I'm walking again, moving.

The windows of the dining room also face out toward the trees, the forest. Nothing else is visible from in here. There is a square table in the middle with a place setting at each spot. Jack directs me to my seat. The others are already sitting.

"You have the last chair, Pennies," says Ruth. "Now we feel like a full table."

I don't bother correcting her. It's just *Penny*. One. Not *Pennies*.

Hilbert looks up. He has a warm twinkle in his eye, as if he has a joke he wants to tell only me. A full plate of steaming food is set down in front of me. The rest of the plates are brought out, and each has the exact same portion of meat, roasted potatoes, and vegetables. There's no way I'll be able to finish it. The meat is covered in dark gravy. I haven't had real gravy in years. I can't help myself. I dip my pinky in the edge and bring it to my mouth. It's hot and silky. Such a deep, rich, satisfying flavor.

"Do you like fish?" asks Ruth.

"Tonight is beef, but we do tend to have fish a lot," says Hilbert.

"Sometimes chicken," Ruth interjects. "Pork chops with apple sauce. Steak. Creamed corn. Greek salad. Shepherd's pie. Spaghetti."

"But the fish is superior to all of those," says Hilbert.

"I don't have much of an appetite these days," I say, but I feel my stomach grumble in anticipation.

Pete picks up his cutlery and starts eating. He appears to be half-asleep. It's how he's looked since I've arrived. Eyes heavy and half-shut. No smile or sign of recognition. Ruth is holding up her fork but is talking too much to start eating.

"We can have wine with supper, if we want," she says. "The rule is only one glass per day."

"And, sadly," says Hilbert, "I had mine at lunch."

I bet Hilbert is the kind of man to find comfort in rules and order and structure. I wonder what he did before coming to the residence. I wonder what brought him here.

"You'd better let her eat," says Jack from across the room. "She'd rather eat the food than talk about it."

Ruth finally stabs a piece of meat and puts it in her mouth. I take the opportunity to do the same.

Hilbert was right; it's beef. But it's unlike any beef I've ever had. It's tender and satisfying in a way none of my meals at home were. Beef was never my favorite. I found it to be chewy and taste of minerals. But this is delectable. I can't help but close my eyes. I'm eating a meal that's not red soup or toast and cheese. My mouth salivates as I chew and swallow.

When I open my eyes, I look at Hilbert. He's using his cutlery meticulously, setting his knife down each time before bringing his fork to his mouth. He dabs a spot of gravy from the corner of his mouth with his napkin. His nails are clean and trimmed.

Rules, order, structure, and neatness.

Despite my nerves from earlier, it's soothing to see a group of old people, of my peers, eating together. Not just eating, but savoring their food. I haven't shared a meal with anyone in a very long

time. I can't remember when. All my dinner parties feel from another life. Eating with others, talking, making eye contact, it's such
a fundamental part of being a person. A daily ritual.

I've missed it terribly without even realizing it.

"Glass of wine?" asks Jack.

"I'm not much of a drinker anymore."

"Some wine, please, yes," says Ruth.

Jack shakes his head. "No, Ruth, not you. You already had your
glass, with lunch today."

Ruth giggles. Hilbert doesn't say anything.

"Actually, I guess I could try some," I say. "Why not?"

"White?"

"Sure."

Jack leaves to get the wine.

"It's nice to have you here," Hilbert says as he picks a tiny crumb
off the sleeve of his jacket. "Our seating discrepancy is finally

solved. Our little table feels complete. There's an elegance to the proportion now. The symmetry of four at one table."

I look around at each old, lined face around me. I can only assume, like mine, their hands and teeth don't work as well as they used to. But they're all happily and hungrily chewing and swallowing bite after bite. It's a pleasure, not a chore.

Jack returns with the wine. He sets the glass down in front of me and walks back into the kitchen. A moment after Jack leaves, I sniff the wine, take a tiny sip. It's subtle, dry, exquisite. I slide the rest of the glass in front of Hilbert.

"Lunch was a long time ago," I say to him.

He receives the glass with a humble nod and takes a sip. Ruth opens her eyes and mouth wide in mock outrage and then starts giggling again.

Pete, undistracted, unaware, continues to eat his food.

After our dessert of warm cherry pie, Jack helps me back to my room. He turns off the overhead light and switches on the soft yellow glow of the lamp.

"Thank you," I say.

"You're welcome, Penny," he says. "You need anything else?"

"No, I don't think so."

"Good night," he says. "Sleep well."

As I brush my teeth and put on my nightgown, I'm feeling something I haven't felt in far too long. I feel looked after, cared for. I'm realizing all that I'd lost over these last few years. Such essential qualities: to feel full and warm and part of a group. Even if I don't know them well yet, and I don't, I can't help but feel energized by it. It's such a strange sensation. I figured I'd never have it again.

Before getting into bed, I stand by my window, and I look out at the darkness. Standing here now, I'm having a hard time placing the front entrance in relation to my room, the common room, and the dining room.

My purse is hanging on the back of my chair, and from one of the inside pockets, I remove a ceramic sculpture I've brought from my apartment. The first sculpture I ever made, with the head tilting to one side. I set it on the dresser and tilt my own head to the side, matching the position.

I switch off the lamp, step out of my slippers, and lie down on my back. I pull the heavy duvet up to my chin. The pillow is just the right size, and firm enough to cradle my head.

It's quiet.

I look up at the blank ceiling, the way I used to do most nights back in my apartment. Maybe we did decide on this together. Maybe he did remind me about this place, about his plan for me, before he died. I suppose I could have forgotten. It would have been a while ago. Maybe I shouldn't be upset about it. I should enjoy it. I'm here now. The people are nice. The food tastes good. This bed is comfortable.

That fall could have killed me. I have nothing to complain about.

It is an adventure.

I roll over onto my side, exhale, and give in to a deep, restful sleep.

Sunlight spills in through the window. I feel a wet spot on the pillow with my cheek. I must have been drooling. What time is it? I rub both eyes. I can't remember the last time I've slept through the night. No bathroom trips. No tossing and turning. I'm in the exact same position I was when I fell asleep.

A faint knock on my door.

"Morning, Penny. It's just me," Jack says, stepping into the room.

He's dressed the same as yesterday. White top and bottoms. Scrubs. A stack of crisp folded towels in his arms.

"Dropping these off for you."

He walks into the bathroom and returns empty-handed.

"So, how'd you sleep?"

"Well," I say, swinging my legs out of bed, bringing a hand up to scratch my hair. "Very well. I can't believe it. I'm just waking up."

"That's great. You look rested," he says.

———

My hair feels greasy and disheveled, like a bird's nest.

"When was the last time you had your hair brushed?" he asks.

"I don't know," I say.

It must look awful. I need a bath.

"I'll give it a quick brush," he says.

I flinch when he touches me. I'm reluctant but relent, closing my eyes. With each brushstroke, I feel myself giving in a little more. Giving in to having someone else brush my hair. Giving in to this place. This house. To the food. To the comforts. To the quiet room and warm bed.

"I slept the whole night," I say. "That never happens. No dreams. Just deep, restful sleep."

He has a soft touch and brushes very gently.

"I'm sorry about your fall," he says. "That must have been scary."

When he says it, I become aware again of the spot on my head. The scab. I hadn't thought about it until right now.

"I don't get the point of aging," I say.

"It comes with lots of changes, doesn't it?" he says.

"There's a reason everyone is obsessed with staying young. You're lucky you still are. And now as much as I want to pretend everything's fine, I know it's not. My knee is getting worse. And my memory is starting to fade. I've started forgetting things."

"I'm sorry, Penny," he says.

"I started writing notes to myself to help remember. I get a little confused sometimes."

"It will be better here."

"Better? No, that's the point. I'm too old to get better. I'm too old for anything."

"That's not true. You slept better, didn't you?"

My eyes drift over to the framed photo on the desk that's sitting beside my ceramic sculpture. It's of him. I don't know why I brought it. I could have just left it at the apartment. I had planned to leave it. Did Mike put it in my bag? Did I unpack it?

"Who's that?" Jack asks, noticing my glance.

"That's him," I say.

"The man you lived with? He was an artist, right?"

"Yes. But he didn't believe in marriage. It was too traditional for him. I don't think he believed in much. He became very cynical, and by the end he looked for approval wherever he could find it. He just wanted to fit in. I don't know why that bothers me so much. But it does."

"Relationships are complicated," he says. "Just like families."

I sense he's about to elaborate, tell me more about his own life, but instead he continues brushing.

"There," he says, when finished, stepping back, holding the brush at his side. "That's better. You still have such pretty, soft hair. Come on. Let's go to breakfast. You must be getting hungry."

I am hungry. I'm famished.

I can feel my stomach grumbling as we walk the corridor. I've managed on my own for years, even as my knee worsened, always walking to get my groceries, but after one day in this house it feels normal to hold on to Jack for help. It's a relief. I watch our feet as we step in unison. His white tennis shoes look brand-new, as if they've never been worn outside.

When we turn left, toward the dining room, the hall lights turn on. They must be on a motion sensor. Everyone else is already in the dining room when we arrive at the entrance.

I look to Hilbert's spot at the table first. He's engrossed in a book. He looks up when I sit down. His face brightens, and he nods.

I notice the others have already eaten their breakfast; dirty cutlery and plates licked clean.

"I wanted to let you sleep a bit longer, Penny, so the others ate before you. Hope you don't mind."

"Of course not," I say.

Pete is slumped in his chair. He's having a post-breakfast nap right at the table.

"Another busy day," says Ruth. "No time to waste. We had to go ahead without you. We couldn't wait any longer. Un autre jour. No time like the present. Enjoy breakfast, Pennies."

There's some spilled egg yolk on her shirt. She stands and bows before walking out.

"If I were to stick around, to keep you company while you eat," says Hilbert, setting his books facedown and pushing his glasses onto his head, "would that be okay with you?"

"Yes," I say, realizing he must have been waiting around for me to arrive. "I'd like that."

He doesn't consider Pete, in his current state, company. I'd have to agree. I wonder how old Pete is. He must be very old. Ancient. Over a hundred? It's hard to tell what's going on behind his blank face and tired eyes.

"I like the shape of your cheek," Hilbert says, out of the blue. "I've never seen a cheek like it."

Instinctually, I bring a hand to my face.

No one has ever commented on my cheek before. It's such a specific part for him to notice and like. My smile, yes. My hair. My eyes. But no one has ever said anything about my cheek. I can tell he means it. I don't know how to respond.

"I used to love reading," I say. "Especially novels. My father used to gift me books about biology. And I had a collection of cookbooks. And art books."

"We have time to read here," he says. "We have all the time we need."

"I don't know. It's not just needing time. The desire seems to have left me. I have a hard time concentrating. I never thought I would lose the ability to do something as simple as following a story or focusing on words on a page. What are you reading?"

He fumbles with his book for a moment. His hands are old, like mine, but his fingers are elegant and slender like a pianist's.

"Um, let's see . . . It's called . . ."

He holds it up for me to read, and I have to lean closer.

Noncommutative Geometry and Number Theory: Where Arithmetic Meets Geometry and Physics

"I don't think I know that one," I say.

We both chuckle. Pete looks up, very briefly, but doesn't make any sign of recognition.

"One of the authors is this wonderful Italian mathematician, Matilde Marcolli."

"I think I probably know more Italian artists than Italian mathematicians," I say. "The names of artists used to mean something to me."

"They don't anymore?"

"It's hard to care in the same way," I say. "It's impossible to be that excited forever."

"Forever is a long time. Earlier I was reading about infinity," he says, "so I do understand. How long is forever?"

"The idea of infinity makes me anxious. And uncomfortable. It always has. I'm a worrier, and anything to do with forever scares me."

"Unless we could live forever," he says.

"Yes, and let Shelley worry about all the details," I say.

"That's right," he says, chuckling. "A forever's worth of toast and eggs."

"If we could stay young, we'd have nothing to be anxious about. Aging is frightening."

"I'm a mathematician," he says. "I don't worry much. There are rules and limits and horizons even if we can't reach them all ourselves."

"I was never any good at math," I say.

Hilbert points to an ancient paint stain on my sleeve that I didn't even realize was there. I cover it with my hand.

"A painter," he says.

"Not anymore. I used to paint. But I've never sold a painting in my life. Or had an opening."

He looks at me attentively.

"That doesn't matter. You paint. You create. You think independently. You're an artist."

———

When was the last time I held a brush?

"I never felt like calling myself an artist. It never had any impact on my work. It's just a label."

"I hope you don't mind if I call you an artist. I could never do what you do," he says. "I think it's wonderful and mysterious."

"I could never do what you do, either," I say.

He grins, mostly with his eyes.

"I have to confess," he says, "I can appreciate art, but I don't always trust myself that I'm getting from it what the artist has intended."

"There isn't only one thing to get. The art I used to do is about layers, a transfer."

"A transfer?"

"From something I experience, something I feel, into something I'm able to produce. Maybe it makes others feel a similar way. Maybe not. I don't know how to explain it beyond that."

"Now that you say it, pure math, algebra, number theory, it's really a system of transferring, too. A solution arrives from a calculation."

"But I don't understand it," I say. "That's not the way my mind works."

"Then I guess you'll just have to trust me," he says.

I do. I trust him. A kind of trust I haven't felt in a very long time: immediate, irrational, impulsive.

Jack sets my plate of breakfast down in front of me. The food is arranged in a happy face. Two fried eggs as eyes, an orange-slice nose, toast ears, and a bacon smile.

"And I'll get you some tea," Jack says.

"Thank you," I say.

Jack walks back to the kitchen.

"Once I had a friend tell me that her garden felt like a three-dimensional painting," I say to Hilbert. "I understood why that would appeal to her, but I didn't care about three dimensions in my work. I already live in three dimensions. That's exactly why I liked painting. I wanted to try to exist only in two dimensions."

"Can you remember why you started?" he asks.

"Painting?"

"Yes."

"Color. I started painting because I loved color. It was that simple. And I like that paintings can change."

"Your paintings change?"

"For me, they all do," I say. "That's what I mean by a transfer. At the start, I have an idea for it, my own idea, certain feelings I'm trying to convey, but at some point, it feels like I give away possession of it, or lose it, and then it's its own thing. I keep seeing it differently."

"The work changes as you change?"

"Yes, it does. Truly. I'm different, and so are my paintings each time I see them. It's an ongoing disruption over time. It's purely emotional. My perspective changes, and that's what painting is about. Perspective and ways of seeing. I hope that doesn't sound too pretentious."

"It doesn't. Not at all."

"All the paintings I've worked on look different to me now. What I feel when I look at them, if I look at them, has transformed from when I started. I haven't thought about this in a long time. I haven't even painted anything in . . ." I trail off.

"How long?"

"I'm not sure. I can't remember the last time I started something new. It became too hard to start. I doubt I'll ever paint again," I say.

"Would you be okay with that?"

I consider the prospect of never painting again. This would have been unheard of for most of my life. It would have felt unjust, a personal tragedy. I wouldn't have accepted it.

"I don't know. Maybe not. I'm feeling different since I've arrived here."

He smiles at this. "I still have lots of work to do."

"You do," I say, hoping not to sound too surprised.

"Yes, work just feels so ingrained now. Even more since I've been here. It's who I am, and she wants us—likes us to stay productive."

I hadn't realized but I must have been eating as we chatted. My plate is empty. The only thing left are two orange rinds.

"If it's not an imposition, I'd like to watch you sometime," he says. "Watch you paint."

I cough when he says this and look away. Jack walks in to clear my plate.

"More tea?"

"No, thank you," I say.

He sets my cutlery on the plate and carries it back to the kitchen. And again Hilbert and I are left in the quiet.

"I was scared of becoming an old person. Terrified. I guess I still am. I was so scared of losing parts of myself and running out of time," I say. "Of forgetting."

Pete hasn't said anything. I forgot he was sitting here with us, but I notice him looking toward the kitchen now, as if he's expecting another plate of food.

"Does getting closer to the end scare you?" I ask Hilbert.

"Why is anything scary?" says Hilbert. "It can only be scary if it's inescapable."

"Like us getting to the end," I say.

"Are we?" he says. "Pete's still here. We're all still here. Shelley keeps telling us day after day that the secret to longevity is for us to stay positive and productive. Positive and productive. Positive and productive."

"How long have you been here?" I ask.

But Hilbert is looking at Pete, who is still staring at the kitchen.

"Pete, do you want something from the kitchen?" Hilbert asks him.

"Do you want me to call Jack?" I ask.

Pete looks at me with his heavy eyes. But he doesn't reply.

I wonder where he came from. I wonder what he's thinking about.

"A man of few words," says Hilbert. "Nothing wrong with that."

"Back at my apartment," I say, "I would go for weeks without talking to anyone. Even when I'd walk out to the park to sit on a bench. Lots of people would go by. Or be in line at the store."

"No one talks to the old folks," he says.

"We're invisible," I say.

The solitary days slipped by one after the other after the other. I saw a mouse once in my apartment. It stopped halfway across the living room and stared at me. I looked down at the small creature. It wasn't scared. We were just both there at the same time. I didn't scream. I didn't react at all. I didn't care about it. If that mouse continued to live in my apartment, to thrive, to mate, scurrying around, eating my crumbs, shitting in the cupboards, or if it died and started to rot in the wall that same night, I didn't care either way. It didn't matter to me. Alive or dead, it was there, in the wall, and it felt the same way about me.

"Are you okay?" asks Hilbert.

"I'm sorry. I was just thinking."

"About what?"

"That it's different here. The food. And the company," I say. "I like it. It's nice."

Jack helps Pete up and asks if I can get back to my room on my own.

"Of course," I tell him.

I already know the route between my room and where we eat. I'm feeling invigorated from my chat with Hilbert. What a morning it's been. So much has happened. Already. It feels like I just woke up. So much has changed for me in such a short time. I feel a connection forming to the others who live here. I'm part of a group now, a community.

I walk into my room to see the light from the window spilling onto my bed. I take another step, then stop.

Sitting on my desk is a brand-new set of paints and a tin of brushes.

I walk closer. All of my favorite colors: ultramarine blue, burnt umber, alizarin crimson, cadmium red. My chest tightens as I stand over them. Something clicks inside of me. A long-forgotten buzz of potential, the same feeling from long ago.

How did these paints get here?

I reach out, lightly running my fingers along the tin and then the brushes themselves. I've painted for most of my life. For most of that time, it filled me with the thrill of possibility. It was an excitement I kept chasing, a feeling I couldn't find anywhere else. A longing.

I loved starting a new portrait. For each one, the process would begin long before I would get my paints out. I wouldn't tell anyone about it. First, I would spend hours sitting outside in the park, sketching whatever I would see. Sometimes this stage would last for weeks. He didn't understand and would ask why I was spending all my time in the park instead of painting.

"No matter what you tell yourself, sketching in the park isn't portraiture," he said.

But to me it was. It was a vital step. I couldn't skip it, and I couldn't rush it. I enjoyed each stage of a piece equally.

Except finishing. I could never finish. I hated trying to complete a piece. It seemed so final. I used to wonder if they had to be finished at all.

"Of course they do," he said. "You can't start something new with-out finishing. You have to learn to make decisions and be ruthless with yourself."

Why couldn't it always be a work in progress? Why not let it remain forever unfolding? To keep that transfer going. Framing a finished painting on a wall was never my objective.

Steps in the hall, and then Shelley appears at the door, intruding on my daydream. I haven't seen her since yesterday. There's a lot I could tell her, about how much I ate and how I talked with Hilbert.

"Penny? Sorry to interrupt, but we're meeting now."

How long have I been standing here?

I see that the light from the window has moved from my bed to my dresser. How did this happen? It is already afternoon? This can't be right.

Shelley sees the bewilderment on my face and steps closer.

"Here, Penny," she says. "It's okay. Take my arm."

As I do, I notice she's wearing gloves. Clear, thin, plastic gloves on both her hands.

L ike they were at breakfast, the others are here before me, waiting, sitting in the same seats from yesterday. Ruth is whistling. Pete and Hilbert sit quietly. Unlike yesterday, today's group meeting feels familiar to me, habitual, normal. Jack leans against the wall, looking down at the phone in his hand.

"I hope everyone's getting excited for the party," says Shelley, once she's seated in her chair.

"We love a party. Love it. They're always fun. Doesn't matter what kind of party. Big, small. We all have to get there for the start and we can't leave until the end. We don't want to miss any of it. No excuses. Maybe we can convince him," Ruth says, pointing at Pete, "to play for us."

It's hard for me to follow everything Ruth says because she speaks so fast, so enthusiastically, occasionally adding the odd French word as she goes.

"I think that's a great idea, Ruth," says Shelley.

Ruth giggles.

"I know," Shelley continues, "that Pete's been practicing a lot. He's amazingly dedicated."

No response from poor, old Pete. I've heard about the very elderly who lose the ability to speak. I wonder what he would say to me if he could still talk. I wonder what his voice would sound like, his laugh.

The more I hear Shelley speak, the more I notice a formal intensity in how she communicates. Everything she says sounds almost scripted and rehearsed.

"I used to dance," I say. It comes out before I know what I'm saying. Everyone, except for Pete, turns toward me. "That was years and years ago. I haven't danced in so long. I don't know if it's even possible at this age, but I have so many fond memories of dancing."

"Dancing *is* fun," says Ruth. "We love it. It takes two to tango."

"I just . . . I hope I still can."

I rub my knee, glancing at Hilbert, and see that he's already looking at me, smiling, eyes twinkling.

"Of course you can still dance," says Shelley.

"We all can," says Ruth.

"I remember attending my first dance in high school, how nervous I felt," I say. "In my twenties I would go out dancing with one friend in particular. We'd dance for hours. I used to dance with lots of men back then. Different men. I could always find them. I felt confident on the dance floor. There were halls that you could go to."

I can hear the music in my head. It's so clear. "Duke Ellington was my favorite," I say. "And Annette Hanshaw. I was so young."

Before I know what I'm doing, I'm humming Annette Hanshaw's version of "Love Me Tonight." I make it through the first few lines and then stop abruptly, mortified that everyone's sitting there listening to me, watching me. What made me speak so openly about something so personal?

"Tu es très jolie," Ruth says to me. "C'est vrai."

"Ruth," says Shelley, "it's still Penny's turn to tell us a story."

"No, no," I say. "It's okay. I prefer hearing Ruth speak French. I spoke a bit of French when I was young. I thought it was very romantic, and I wish I'd kept it up."

"I was hoping you might find things in common with the others," says Shelley. "And with me. The way you appreciate art, Penny, is the way I appreciate the human body. Even as a young girl, I was obsessed with learning everything I could about anatomy and the science of life."

"What did you want, Penny?" asks Hilbert abruptly. "When you were young."

Shelley looks surprised that Hilbert has cut her off.

"What do you mean?" I ask.

"I mean, what did you want out of life?"

"That's a big question," I say.

"The biggest," he says.

"Well, I suppose I wanted to get out of my own little world," I say. "To see art. I wanted to read and meet people. I wanted to grow up so I could learn to paint."

Hilbert is quiet. Eventually, he says, "When I was a young man I wanted to fully understand set theory and the possible sizes of infinite sets. Such a breathtaking mystery."

His answer makes me laugh.

———

"That's silly," says Ruth, rolling her eyes.

"No, it's not," I say. "Not at all. I'm always trying to understand how to end my work. That's my version of infinity."

I haven't known this man for long, but I can picture him then, still an undergrad. Modest, intelligent, lanky, preoccupied, handsome. And brilliant.

"I like that your version of infinite sets is completely different to mine," I say.

"I've already learned a lot from you," says Hilbert.

"Hardly," I say.

But Hilbert reaches over and places a hand gently atop mine. It's the first time he's touched me. His hand is warm, heavy, comforting. Shelley notices his gesture.

"I think it's time to—" Shelley starts saying, but I cut her off.

"I remember something else," I say.

"Pardon?" she says.

"That I wanted. When I was very young. A little girl. Before I started painting or before I went out dancing. I wasn't very social as a child. A lot of things scared me. But I remember wanting something in a serious way. I didn't even tell my parents. I've never told anyone."

"What was it?" asks Hilbert.

"I wanted to levitate. To float."

"You wanted to fly?" says Ruth.

"No. To *float*," Hilbert says, clarifying for me. "She said she wanted to float."

"That's an unusual wish," says Shelley.

"I wanted to know what that would feel like," I say.

Shelley looks at me and then at the others. Jack still hasn't moved from the wall, but he's not looking down at his phone anymore. I can tell he's listening.

"Just to float, just for a moment," I say, looking down. "To feel my feet off the ground. I've always felt my weight. It's impossible to know what it would feel like until you feel it."

My little childhood secret is met by silence, except from Hilbert.

"It's an understandable anxiety of matter, of mass," says Hilbert. "Of life. A density. A burden to remain upright, to produce, to persist. I've felt it, too."

I feel the hairs on my arms rise.

"There's nothing wrong with persistence, Hilbert," says Shelley. "That's what life is. That shows a strong spirit."

"No, that's not what we're talking about," Hilbert says to Shelley, before turning back to me. "Some have argued that the total amount of energy, all of it, in the universe is . . . do you want to guess? It's zero."

"That doesn't sound possible," says Shelley.

"Shhh," I say before focusing my attention back on Hilbert.

"All matter makes up the positive energy, while gravity makes up the negative energy, and the two, put together, just cancel each other out," he says.

Shelley scoffs under her breath.

"Yes. I see. It's about being different. Being completely different," I say. "The other side of something. I find it very soothing to know that an opposite always exists."

I'm looking only at Hilbert. He's all I can see. I smile.

"Isn't common ground the most important thing?" Shelley says. "Integrating and coming together for the good?"

"I find contrasts soothing, too, Penny," Hilbert says, ignoring Shelley. "I like knowing there's a flip side. I think it's beautiful. It's not unlike floating. A balance and proportion."

"Anyway, let's not get too philosophical," Shelley says, standing up. "You never cease to amaze me. All of you!" Her tone is pointed, as if we've touched a nerve. "But you all need your rest, too. Jack, can you help Penny back to her room?"

"Now?" he asks, surprised.

"Yes, now."

Jack steps forward and puts his arm out for me to hold on to. The room has gone quiet. I want to continue talking with Hilbert, ask him questions about his life, his work in mathematics, his ideas, other interests. It's all so different from my own, and yet . . . I take hold of Jack's arm and stand.

"We're lucky to be here, aren't we?" I say to Hilbert, as I pass.

"Lucky, yes," he says. "It seems that way today."

"What's that, Hilbert? It seems what way?" Shelley asks.

There's an edge to her question that pricks me like the sharp quill of a feather. From the doorway, I hear Hilbert's response.

"I didn't mean anything," he says. "I'm just happy Penny's here."

I let go of Jack's arm as we walk along the hall to my room.

"It's okay," I say. "I know the way."

"And your knee?"

"It still works," I say. "For now."

We pass the window facing the dense forest. We stop for a moment, standing side by side. There are so many tall, indistinguishable trees out there, too many to count. I try looking at one tree in particular, focusing intently, until I forget what I'm looking at.

"I liked what you were saying in there, about feeling your own weight," he says, breaking the spell. "I think you and I have a few things in common."

"Is that right?"

The sound of Shelley's footsteps down the hall cause Jack to stop what he's saying. He waits until we hear a door close.

"I was in art school once," he says, his voice softer now, quieter, as if it's a secret.

"You studied art?"

"At college. Only for a year. Feels like another life."

"Why only a year?"

"It didn't work out," he says.

"Why?"

"I wasn't ready for it," he says. "I made some mistakes. Flunked out. I always thought I would be a professional artist. That was going to be my identity. But now I'm here. Working at a place like . . ."

He stops himself from finishing his thought.

A place like this?

"Don't you like it here?" I ask.

"It's a good place to be. It's just not what a young Jack saw himself doing, that's all."

He is still young, I think. I turn away from the window first and start walking again. Jack follows.

"Well," I say. "I never studied art at all. Not formally. So you have a leg up on me. A good leg, not an old, arthritic one like mine."

We reach my room with the red door. It now has *Penny* written on a little hanging sign. That's new. We walk in, and I sit down in my chair.

"For the last few years at my apartment, I felt like I'd missed my chance. That everything was done. No more experiences. No more challenges. No new relationships. It's a scary feeling when it's all over. Especially when you're alone."

I'm trying desperately to hold it in, but Jack realizes my eyes are welling up.

"I'm sorry," I say.

"Don't apologize," he says.

I take a moment to compose myself.

"What is it?" he asks. "What's wrong?"

"Nothing. That's exactly it. Nothing's wrong here. In fact, it's the opposite. It's really nice."

I remove a balled-up tissue from the sleeve of my sweater, blow my nose.

"For the first time in ages, I feel good. I've slept. I've eaten. I've talked with other human beings my own age. It feels wonderful. It's a little overwhelming, that's all. And all in one day."

He puts a hand on my shoulder.

I use my finger to wipe the tears from my cheek. I walk farther into the room. I sit down in my chair with an exhale. I close my eyes, resting my head back. I sit like this until I remember what was on my desk this morning.

"Jack, where did the new paint and brushes come from?" I ask, opening my eyes.

But he's not here. He is already gone.

When I wake, I'm still in the chair. My head is tilted back and to the side. My feet are up on the footrest. There's a blanket over my legs and a glass of water on the side table. It must have been a long nap. When did I decide to take a nap?

And then I notice: Shelley is in here with me.

She's in the corner of the room, just standing there. She's changed out of her red dress into a more casual sweater and jeans. She walks over, reaching down, and very softly touches my cheek with the back of her hand, the way a parent might do to a young child. The thin, see-through glove she's wearing is cool on my skin. Clammy.

"You looked so peaceful. I didn't want to disturb you."

I try to swallow. "How long have I been asleep? I'm very thirsty," I say.

"Here," she says, handing me the water. She watches while I drain the entire glass.

"We have a treat lined up for you tomorrow morning. You're going to have a spa day."

I hand the empty glass back to her.

"A what day?"

"Spa. Get your hair washed and cut, nails done."

I look down at my dirty, jagged nails.

"Only if it's not an inconvenience," I say.

"Not in the least. It will be good for the party," she says. "You'll love it. But first, it's time for your shower."

The hot water is sublime. I let it fall over my head, neck, and face. I needed this, badly. It's rejuvenating. I just wish I could be in here on my own, to have some privacy.

Shelley insisted on helping me. She's removed her shoes and has put a white water-resistant robe on over her clothes. She stands off to the side of the giant shower stall, while I'm in the stream of hot water.

"I'm fine to do this on my own," I say. "There was no one to help me at my apartment."

"I know, my dear. But that's why you're here, remember—to get help."

The water pressure is much stronger than back home and stings my skin in a pleasant way. I feel Shelley step closer. She picks up a washcloth and starts scrubbing my back. The material of her robe feels like a rain jacket against my skin.

"Hold your arms up, please."

I do, and she washes there. I don't look back. It's awkward and embarrassing. I've never been washed before, at least not as an adult. I don't know Shelley yet, not really. I wish I couldn't see her bare feet. For some reason that makes it worse. They're almost touching mine. We aren't talking. The water is hot and steams around us.

Without saying anything, without pausing her movements, Shelley starts humming. Subtly at first. I barely hear her over the running water. Then louder. I know the tune. I recognize it. It's the same one I was humming earlier, at the meeting.

It's an old Annette Hanshaw song. It's from before her time.

She continues humming as she washes the rest of the soap off my body. For the first time since I've arrived, I wish I was alone.

She turns off the water and hands me a fluffy towel.

"Would you like help drying off?"

"No," I say.

"I'll get your nightie."

"Is it time for bed already?"

From where I'm standing in my bathroom, I can see through the open door to the window. I step closer, putting a hand on the doorframe. It's dark outside. I can hear Shelley opening my dresser drawer. It must be later than I think.

Once I get my nightie on, again with her help, Shelley tucks me into bed.

"I didn't realize it was so late," I say. "I guess that nap was a long one. Did we already have dinner?"

"I'm pleased you're settling in. And sleeping so well," she says. "That's important."

She has removed the white shower robe but is still wearing those gloves. The bed, with the duvet up under my chin, is just as warm and comfortable as I recall from last night. I am sunken and protected. I close my eyes and can feel myself drifting off immediately.

"Good night, my dear," I hear. "Sleep well."

I open my eyes. Sit up. It's dark. It's late. Where am I?

I remember. My room at Six Cedars. I don't have a watch. I didn't bring my bedside clock. It must be the middle of the night. There's no sound. No light shining in from the hallway. Everyone is asleep.

But I feel awake. I feel alert.

I get up. To paint. I want to paint. I need to paint.

Without putting on my cardigan or socks or slippers, I go straight to my desk. That's where my new brushes are. I pick up one of the brushes. I touch the soft tip with my finger. I sniff it.

I turn on the desk lamp, and for the first time in years, I start work on a new canvas.

I don't know how long I work like that, barefoot, focused, but at some point I become exhausted and fall back into bed.

A noise. It's a voice. Soft. Muffled. Someone's speaking to me.

"Penny . . . Penny?"

I open my eyes. It's Jack, standing over my bed. He's holding fresh folded towels. Again.

"Good morning," he says.

I feel muddled, disoriented. It takes me a moment to assess: sunlight gently shining into the room, trees outside my window, my body under the blanket. It must be morning.

"How'd you sleep?" he says. "Just dropping these for you."

His eyes are baggier than yesterday. Darker. He looks different.

"I . . . slept fine," I say, bringing a hand to my head. "How about you?"

I glance at my desk. The canvas from last night isn't there. I must have put it away. I must have hid it, and I'm thankful that I did. My work has always been private but especially when I've just started a piece.

"I'm supposed to take you down to the spa after you've had breakfast."

I muster a small nod of acceptance.

In the dining room, Jack tells me that the others already finished, that I slept in. I miss eating with the group. Especially Hilbert. I was looking forward to seeing him. When I'm done with my breakfast, Jack clears my plate, and instead of going back to my room, we walk the opposite way down the hallway, to a room I've never been in.

It looks like a makeshift salon, with a large mirror mounted on the wall, a sink with a spout, and a swivel chair.

"What's the smell?" I ask.

"Aromatherapy. Helps the body get rid of toxins," he says.

Jack eases me into a chair in front of a basin. The spout has a long handle.

"We'll start with a wash. Lean back, relax."

He places a small towel around my shoulders and carefully leans my head back toward the basin. He cradles my head with one hand, and with the other, he holds the spout over my hair. I feel the warm water on my scalp.

First the shower last night with Shelley, and now he's washing my hair. I was neglecting these parts of healthy living, letting myself go to seed. The warmth from the water spreads from my head to my hair to my body and into my arms. I have goose bumps.

I close my eyes.

I wonder what Ruth is doing now. Napping in her room? And Pete? They're all here in the house with me. They must all get a turn in here, in this chair, too, getting their hair washed like this. Does it feel as nice for them as it does for me? Do they need it as much as I do?

I hear Jack set the spout down in the basin and click open the shampoo bottle. He starts gently massaging it into my hair and scalp.

"I've been thinking," he says.

The way he's rubbing my head feels calming, tranquilizing.

"You should get someone to sit for you. For a portrait."

"What?"

"I'm serious."

I think about telling him what happened in the middle of the night, how I got out of bed feeling inspired and alert. I got my new paints out. I started work. But I don't feel ready to share that yet.

"It's been a long time," I say. "The stuff I do is not typical. I wouldn't want to shock anyone."

"From the pieces I've seen, I love your style. The one you have with the pair of eyes touching. It's amazing. I was into surrealism, too. Yours have this dreamlike quality I can relate to."

I assumed that piece had been put in storage. It's one of my oldest.

"When did you see that painting?" I ask.

"When you arrived. I carried your things and unpacked for you. I couldn't resist looking at some of the paintings. I hope you don't mind."

"No, I don't," I say. "It's just . . . I didn't know that one was here."

"When I came to get you out of bed this morning, you were sleeping so soundly. I think you were dreaming, because I could see your eyes twitching. I wanted to give you a bit more time to rest, so I went into your closet and had a look at that painting again. I'd been thinking about it a lot since first seeing it. It's a beautiful piece, Penny, because it's—"

"It's very old," I say sharply. "And it's not finished. It's not meant to be seen."

"But I really like it."

I hold them too close, I think. My paintings. I always have. "It's unusual for me to get a compliment like this," I say. "I shouldn't be so sensitive. Thank you."

"I'm thinking you could do one . . . of us . . . the staff or the residents. Ruth maybe. Or Hilbert."

"I don't know about that."

"I hope you don't mind me saying this, Penny, but you actually remind me a bit of my mom."

"Really? Are the two of you close?"

"We were. She had a spark, like you. Everyone noticed it. A curiosity about life. She saw things differently."

"Do you get to see her much?"

"She passed away when I was young."

"I'm so sorry," I say. "How old were you?"

"Seventeen when she died. It's like you said, Penny, all families are complicated."

Did I say that?

"My mother was sweet but not always present. It was my father who used to wash my hair," I say, as my own memory returns. "When I was really young, I mean. He'd make a shield with his hand in the shape of a crescent moon and hold it to my forehead so I wouldn't get any soap in my eyes."

I can't believe I remember this. I rarely have memories of my father. He wasn't always easy, but he was tender. He tried his best.

Jack shields my eyes from the soapy water. We've gone quiet, the two of us, lost in thought. All I hear is the running water. After a minute or two, I realize the water is still running, but Jack's hand is not on me anymore.

"There's nothing as comforting as hot, soapy water," I hear.

It's her. Shelley.

I open my eyes. My head is still tilted back, and I look up toward the ceiling, her face hovering over mine. She's wearing eyeliner, and I can smell her perfume.

"I love your hair," Shelley says. "It is so soft."

She continues rinsing my hair as she talks. Her touch is firmer, not quite as gentle as Jack's.

"Where's Jack?" I ask.

"He's around somewhere. Penny, you're so impressive to me," she says. "So independent, so strong."

"I'm not sure you can say that about an old lady who needs help washing."

"We all need help. None of us can do anything without others. It's your spirit I'm talking about. Your attitude. And your work ethic. Your painting."

"My painting?"

"I saw what you're working on. You're so talented."

My heart stops. How could she have seen it? I only started it last night. And I hid it, didn't I? I don't like this. It's an intrusion.

"You looked at my painting?" I ask.

She nods.

"It's personal," I say. "Private."

"We don't like to have secrets here. We're such a small group, and I want to know all about you."

She wraps my hair in a towel. It's constricting and pulling at my hair. She wheels my chair to the mirror on the wall.

She knows so much about me, my work, my life. But I know nothing about her.

"Who are you?" I ask.

She takes a step backward, her head cocked to one side. "What do you mean?"

"Jack told me a bit about you. He said you were an academic. How does an academic end up managing an old-age home?"

I can tell from her expression that Jack wasn't supposed to tell me this.

"We're not an old-age home, Penny. We're a small-scale assisted-living facility. And I'm not sure what Jack's been saying. Before I started Six Cedars, I studied science."

"What kind of science?"

"Organic chemistry, biology. If you'd asked me in grad school what I wanted to do with my life, I would have said become a speculative biologist."

"Speculative biologist? My father loved to read about science and would often buy me books on various topics, but I've never heard of that."

"Biology in particular is very under-theorized. It's still mainly based in observation and experiment. I'm more attracted to the theoretical."

"The theoretical?" I say.

"Especially when it comes to boundaries. The natural world is much more lax about borders than people think." She sounds excited, candid, much less formal than she has since I've arrived.

"How so?" I ask.

"Well, there are so many examples. Do you know what lichens are?"

"That green stuff that grows on tree bark?"

"Yes, but lichen isn't a singular entity. They're a symbiotic fusion of algae and fungi. It's amazing. But their union is so extreme that they perform as one, as lichens."

Symbiotic fusion?

"Perform as one?" I ask, struggling to follow her thought flow.

"As in one individual. And so when you start getting deeper into it, you wonder if you should be discussing a single organism or many. Is it *me* or is it *us*? It's like reindeer cyclones. Are they one or many? A swirling group of reindeer walking in a tight circle, which they'll do if threatened, so any one individual can't be targeted. Imagine if we could all be linked like this, how much better off we'd be."

I suddenly picture walking in a tight circle with Hilbert and Ruth and Pete, the four of us huddled together, back-to-back-to-back-to-back, for our own protection.

As she's talking, she picks up a blow-dryer, turns it on, and starts drying my hair, brushing it out.

———

Why didn't Jack finish doing my hair? Why did he leave me? Why did they switch? She never even said where he went. I feel a pit open in my stomach.

"How did you end up here? Doing this work?" I ask.

"My grandparents owned this house. My parents inherited it from them, and they used it as a summer house. I loved coming here as a child. It felt like a mansion out of a movie. I had so much fun here during those long summers, but I was always alone, and I would imagine what it would be like to have friends here with me. . . ."

She trails off, and I feel myself shiver.

"The days and years go by so fast," she says. "I wish there was a way to slow everything down, don't you? To have more time. Time is the most important thing."

She sets the blow-dryer down and picks up a comb and a pair of scissors.

My eyes wander to the mirror. Beside it are two plastic bins. One appears empty, the other has hair clippings in it.

"I guess everyone would like more time," I say. "I might have given a different answer before I got here. But more time would be good now."

I think about what more time would actually mean. For me, Pete, Ruth, Hilbert. More sitting around. More eating. More sleeping. I would get to paint more. But what would the work mean if it was endless? What would a relationship mean if it kept going forever? What would a day be if it didn't end?

More and more and more and more and more and more and more and more and more and more and more and more and more and more and more and more.

It's what everyone wants, so she says.

"What if time was all you had?" I say. "Maybe if we had all the time in the world, life would start to feel meaningless. Or worse."

The scissors she's using to cut my hair aren't new. They make a hard swish sound each time they snip.

"No, Penny," she says. "You're wrong about that. Don't say that again, please."

I look down at my lap.

"More time can only be good," she goes on. "It's our duty to form connections and make strong links while we can. There is nothing wrong with dependence and asking for help. There is strength in fitting in, in sacrificing your identity as an individual, in becoming part of something bigger than just yourself."

My hair falls off and down to the floor at her feet. She's trimming it, cutting it in a simple, plain bob style.

She never asked me how I wanted it cut. She never asked.

"When I was young, I loved getting my hair cut," she says. "I loved knowing that it would grow back. No matter what. We should always have elegant, well-maintained hair. It's part of who we are."

I watch her in the mirror. She pauses, steps back, looks down at my hair, the scissors at her side.

"I'm glad you've enjoyed talking with Hilbert," she says to me in the mirror.

I feel myself blush.

"He's a sweetheart, isn't he? He's brilliant, you know. Still works on his equations every day. We encourage all of you to have something to focus on, to make use of your time here. It's a special group we have."

Shelley makes eye contact again, through the mirror, then continues cutting.

I never wanted to only have one serious boyfriend. I always said yes to dates. I loved meeting new boys. Even if we just went out once or twice. I'd always give them a chance. All my friends seemed ready for marriage and kids right away. Not me.

And then I met someone. I met him at one of his openings. He was outgoing and articulate. I could tell he felt something for me, and I liked how confident he seemed. Within two months, we'd decided to move in together.

I didn't know then that I would spend the rest of my adult life with him. Until coming here.

I have a hard time remembering more than that. We did fall in love. We did have fun, for a while. It's so strange. All that time together and I'm left with only a vague feeling about facts and details.

"Hilbert is easy to talk with," I say. "He waits to be asked questions before he gives his thoughts. He wants to ask me about mine. I think he and I are very different. I don't understand the world the way he does, and I really like that. Too often I've only been around other artists. I trust him."

"It sounds to me like you might have a little crush, Penny," Shelley says.

"I'm too old for any of that now."

She starts using a soft brush to remove any stray hairs around my face and neck.

"Give me your hand, please," she says.

I hold my hand up. Shelley takes it and starts to give me a hand massage, rubbing her gloved thumbs over my palm. It's firm but not unpleasant.

"Human touch is so important. You've gone so long without."

She's right. I have. Years. Even when he was still alive, the touch I felt and the touch I gave were mostly cold and brisk. I let my eyes slip shut again. I feel her hold my thumb and then the click of a nail clipper. She's cutting my nails. She's taking her time, doing it meticulously.

"Your nails are like your hair, healthy and strong. We could paint them if you want. Maybe pink? Something fun for the party."

She starts cutting the nails of my left hand. She's cutting the nails quite short.

"I don't paint my nails."

"That's okay."

She cuts another nail, the clippers snapping.

"I never understood the point."

"No problem."

"I bite them."

"You bite your nails?"

"Yes, I always have."

She cuts another nail.

"If you paint them, you just have to do it again when it wears off."

"Whatever you like, my dear."

As she says this, she trims a nail too short, and it stings. I pull my hand away.

"Oh no! I'm sorry. That hurts, doesn't it?"

Shelley takes a step back as I examine my finger. It starts to bleed, just a bit. She takes a hold of the finger and squeezes it, holding it tightly. She dabs it with the end of a Q-tip, which she then drops into the small bin. It's right beside the bin that has the hair clippings in it. It all happens in a blink, and I'm not sure what I've just seen.

———

"At least we know you have good, healthy-looking blood."

I pull my finger back, bringing it up to my mouth. I suck the sore spot, looking at her. The shade of her lipstick is red. Bright red. Brighter than it has been, I think. Did she just put it on?

I feel a drip of sweat fall from my armpit, trickle down my side.

Can one person's blood be more healthy-looking than another's?

With my freshly washed cut hair and trimmed nails, I'm standing at my desk. Shelley brought me back to my room and said I could start working again.

"Your hair looks great," she said as she left. "Good luck."

I bring a hand up to my forehead. Not to touch my hair but to feel the scab from my fall. I haven't thought about it today, and I can feel with my finger that the scab has dried. It's healing. I'm healing. I can still heal, I guess, even at this stage of life.

It's strange how sleeping so well has affected my perception. I have no sense anymore of what a night is. I used to lay awake for so long in the dark that a night would take forever. Now I close my eyes and a moment later I open them to morning.

I also haven't had any dreams since I've been here. Not that I can remember. Just deep, restful, dreamless sleeps.

I refocus on the canvas on my desk. It's liberating to be working again. I feel younger. I have my head down, bent over the desk, when I get the uncomfortable sense of being watched. I stop, put down my brush, and look around my room.

I look behind me, toward my open door. A light in the hallway turns on, as if someone is there. I wait to see if they walk by. No one does. I wait. The cat walks in, rubbing up against my leg. I lean down and rub behind its ears.

He's a cute, wee thing. I can feel his little ribs. He's bordering on gaunt. But he likes when I rub his ears like this. When he scurries out, I look down at the painting, then back up to see Jack standing at my door.

"It's so good to see you working on a new piece," he says, walking in without knocking. "I have something for you. A noise-canceling device, like headphones, that you just slip over your ears. They block out all the background sounds that you've been hearing."

Have I been hearing background sounds? I don't remember saying anything to Jack about hearing sounds. Or to anyone else.

"Like what kinds of sounds?"

"All the old house stuff. Pipes, floorboards—the wood shifts on cold nights. I'll show you how they work. They'll help you concentrate and focus."

He puts the headphones on over my ears and turns them on.

Silence. Not just quiet. It's complete and utter silence.

I've never experienced this before, other than being underwater. Jack starts talking. I see his mouth moving, but I can't hear anything.

He starts moving around the room, tapping the wall, but I don't hear any of it. I'm under the ocean. Or in a dream. It's peaceful, as if I'm hovering in space, but the removal of all sound is also strangely unnerving; to know there's still communication out there directed at me but I'm not able to understand it. To know someone is walking down the hall, but not to hear it. No voices, no steps. No doors opening or closing. No wind through the branches of the trees that I used to love hearing in the park.

I'm not sure if I like it or hate it.

He takes the headphones off me.

"Amazing, right? Everyone else here already has a pair. They love them."

"I think I'd prefer if I could hear music. I used to listen to music all the time."

"These are meant more for cutting out distractions. Ruth uses hers when she's working."

"Working?"

"She translates different texts into English. Mostly from French. She does it for hours at a time."

"Is there any way you could get some music for them? Please."

"I can try, Penny."

Jack walks over to the bed and starts stripping off the sheets.

As I watch him remove the cases from both pillows, it happens again, the way it did when I was getting my hair washed. A memory from childhood returns. Out of the blue. I'm surprised I remember it.

"Whenever my dad would change the sheets of my bed, which probably wasn't all that often, but whenever he did, we had this little game," I say. "I don't know how it started. He would have all the dirty sheets stripped off the bed, lying on the floor in a messy ball, and I would get down under them. I would say to him that there's a delivery for him. And he would then get down and start feeling around with his hands, saying, 'I wonder what it could be,' and I would be trying so hard to hold in my laughter. And then he would finally rip the sheets away and say, 'Oh, it's you.' It was pure joy. Seeing his smiling face. His eyes focused on me. We did it over and over, and the feeling never changed. It was so simple."

Jack walks by with the sheets that he's removed, and without saying anything, he puts one of them over my head playfully.

"What's this weird package?" he says, laughing. "Eh, Penny, what do we have here?"

I'm giggling, too, but then I stop. I stick my head out. I wonder why he's changing the sheets. I've only slept in them twice. "You're washing the sheets?" I ask.

"What?"

"My sheets. Do you think they need to be changed already?"

"We like to keep them clean," he says. "Ruth hates dirty sheets."

He takes one backward step, still looking at me, then, arms full of sheets, he turns and walks out of the room.

The four of us eat in silence. We're savoring yet eating ferociously. A full table again.

I must have worked up such an appetite from painting all afternoon. I was famished by the time our plates were brought out. Famished, and still thinking about Jack's last comment to me.

Why would he tell me that Ruth hates dirty sheets? What does that have to do with me?

Meat and rice in a sweet, sticky sauce. We have warm bread with extra butter on the side. All through the meal, I can't stop peering over at Ruth.

Ruth hates dirty sheets.

Ruth, the language expert. The translator. Jack said she translates for hours at a time. Whenever I've seen her she's been talkative, outgoing, laughing. But tonight she is focused on her meal, like the rest of us.

I try not to make it obvious, but I keep peeking toward her. How she's sitting. The way her short hair is styled. Her smooth complexion. How she holds her fork and the way her lips curl up when she grins. She's so pretty, almost youthful. She looks much younger than me. I wonder how old she is.

When our plates have been cleared, and Jack's back in the kitchen, it's Ruth who reaches over and touches my leg under the table.

"Do you want to go somewhere and talk?" she asks, as if she knows I'd been thinking about her.

"Okay," I say.

Ruth leads us to the chairs in the hallway seating cove. She waits for me to sit before she does, too.

"How long have you been here?" I ask.

Ruth laughs as if it's a silly question.

"Hard to say. Old Pete was the first of us. Then Hilbert. Then you. Now us."

"Us?"

"Here, us. We're all here. We're home now. Finally. For good."

"For good?"

Ruth puts a hand over her mouth as to muffle a laugh and then quickly stands up. She starts walking away. She turns back and motions for me to follow, still chuckling. I get up and follow a few steps behind, watching how her hips sway. When I catch up, she surprises me by taking my arm in hers.

It's like when I used to go dancing with my friend. This is how we'd walk from dance club to dance club. Moving this way, together, I can feel the ease of her steps, me following her lead. She's not as stiff as me.

"Do you find it loud here?" I ask. "Do you hear things?"

"We have the space and time to work," she says. "We're lucky."

She's trying to synchronize our steps as we walk, until our strides are even and we've ended up at the spa room where I had my hair washed. The door is open, but no one is in there. Ruth stops us.

"On the first day, Shelley washes hair."

"Yes," I say. "Did she cut your nails?"

She grins, winks, and directs us in.

Ruth motions for me to sit down in the spa chair.

"Should we be in here?" I ask.

"Pourquoi pas?" She picks up a bottle of nail polish. "For the party," she says.

She's really giggling now as she moves around in front of me.

"Were you ever married, Ruth?"

Ruth has to think about it. "Not yet, but hopefully one day."

"And you don't have any children or family left?"

"Children will come after marriage."

"I don't think any of us have family left. There's no one to check in on us or ask about us. Or visit. Does anyone get any visitors?"

"We're together. We have everything we need right here. Don't you remember painting our nails and putting on makeup when we were young?" she says, holding up her hand to show me her nails. All her nails are painted red like Shelley's. Looking closer, I see that the side of one of Ruth's nails has been cut too short, like my own.

All of a sudden, I can't hear her anymore. I can't hear her words. I can't hear her voice.

Ruth speaks, her mouth moves, but I can't hear any sounds. I bring my hand up to my ear.

Her mouth opens in a laugh, small at first, then wider, but I don't hear it. What's wrong with me? I watch Ruth's mouth opening and closing as my panic grows and swells. My heart beats faster, heavier.

And then, as quickly as it happened, I hear her again.

"What? What's wrong?" Ruth asks. "You look pale."

"It's nothing," I say. "It's . . . I like the color of your nails. Red suits you."

I slowly get up from the chair to stand beside Ruth. We are shoulder to shoulder looking in the mirror.

"This feels good, doesn't it?" she says.

"What?"

My new haircut is so much like hers. I hadn't noticed it until I see us together like this, side by side. I look at my own face, closely, carefully, in a way I haven't looked at myself in many years. I didn't like the old face looking back at me, so at some point, I just stopped looking at it.

But I can see it now. My skin looks better.

It's subtle. Maybe it's because I'm sleeping so well. And eating. We stand, staring at ourselves and each other, until Ruth speaks.

"Do you think he likes us?"

Our feet are so close the sides are touching. She interlocks our arms again.

"Who?" I ask.

She rolls her eyes.

"Hilbert," she says.

"Do you like him?" I ask.

"He's handsome. Definitely smart. Tall, and dresses well. A bit dull, though."

"He's smart in a different way," I say. "Which I like."

"There are worse things than dull."

"You're right about that," I say.

"Like someone who needs to always be reassured all the time, someone who is inward-looking," she says.

"Yes!" I say. "That's right. That's hard to live with for so long."

"It is," she says. "It's exhausting."

"Because," I say, "it gets worse over time, not better. When you're so similar to a partner, there's that risk of it feeling more like cooperation than true appreciation. There needs to be that unending, renewing affection. When the superficial wore off, I didn't feel any wonderment, you know?"

"Yes, we know," she says.

"I stopped being astonished by him. There was no complexity there, only ego."

"Is Hilbert complex, Pennies?"

Before I can answer, we hear something, a door opening, maybe.

"Shhhh," I say. "What was that?"

"Uh-oh. We're not supposed to be in here," Ruth says.

We hear it again.

"I thought you said it didn't matter if we were here."

"No, we can't. We'll be in big trouble. She'll be livid. Let's go," she says, taking my hand.

She's pulling me ahead, into the dark hallway. She puts a finger over her lips, then with a shifty look, winks again and walks back down the hall. I watch her go.

My stomach clenched when Ruth said *She'll be livid*. Her eyes changed. They looked fearful. I wait until I can't hear anything, no steps, no doors. I turn and sneak off the other way.

I tiptoe along the hallway until I pass by the dining room, and when I do, the lights come on. I hear someone in the kitchen. Maybe that's the clang Ruth and I heard. She must have gone back to her room. I know I should just keep going, go back to my room, but I hear the noise again. There are many sounds in an old house like this. That's just what Jack said.

I step slowly through the empty dining room, one hand touching the wall for support. It's not as cozy when it's empty and dark. I feel a draft as if a window is open. I get to the door of the kitchen. I push my hand against it, curious where the noise is coming from, and the door opens, just a crack. There's barely enough space for me to see inside.

I open the door wider and step in. The light doesn't come on automatically. It's dark, but I can make out a long counter, shelves holding pots, pans, and plates. I had no idea the kitchen was this large. It seems to keep going and going. Why doesn't the light come on? I wave my hand, hoping that will flip the sensor. But it doesn't.

I hear the noise again, look up and see movement at the end of the kitchen. I see a person. It's Jack.

He has his back to the door, so he doesn't see me. I take two indecisive steps toward him. He suddenly swings around to face me. His white shirt is unbuttoned. It's sweaty, and he has something in his hand. He's holding a glass of wine.

"Jack?"

I step closer, trying to see better. He's muttering to himself under his breath.

"All I do is work, work, work. Every day. She's obsessed. For what? I don't even go outside. But I have no other options."

He looks aghast, panicked, ashamed.

"I started working here, thinking it would be temporary. But it's not. I can't leave!"

He sees me. He looks right at me.

"I'm a coward," he says. "We're all cowards. We're all scared of the same thing."

"What are we scared of?" I ask.

He wipes at his face. He's crying. I shouldn't see this. I shouldn't be in here.

Jack downs the rest of the glass. And then he laughs. It's more a snicker, but it's a strange sound, like pain. An injured animal. His eyes are dark. His face is unreadable. I try, but I can't speak. I can't make a sound.

What are we sacred of? I try to say again, but this time I can't get it out. I stomp my foot, hoping it will reverberate, but it doesn't.

I turn and walk out as fast as I can.

Outside the kitchen, through the dining room, I walk back along the hallway. This is not the comfortable, cozy place I thought it was. I was wrong about that, fooled. With each step, each pulse, I can feel my heart beating faster, harder. I keep walking, trying to steady myself. I don't want them to see my unease. I want to hide it. I look at the walls around me, the ceiling and floor. They don't look the same as when I was just here with Ruth. The walls have changed. So have I.

I tap my knuckle against the wall, and thankfully, it makes the familiar sound of bone on wood. I can hear my own steps again as I walk. I get back to my room, enter, and close the door. I stand in the dark, with my back against the door, looking at my big, comfortable bed. It's calling to me.

I feel my heart rate lower, my breath slow.

I lie down on the bed, get under the covers, and close my eyes.

My mind is racing. I'm too anxious to go to sleep. So much has happened. And all . . . tonight? First, dinner, then the talk with Ruth. Seeing Jack in that desperate state. Him seeing me. The look on his face. Is Hilbert asleep in his room?

Ruth said something about Shelley being livid if she found us in the spa. Jack said she's obsessed. With what?

Where is Shelley? Where does she go at night?

There's a dull ache in my temples. I'm sweating. I feel hot in one moment, cold the next. I sit. I stand. I pace around my room. What was Jack doing in there?

I should have stayed longer, tried to help him. He was so upset. But I couldn't speak. I couldn't make a sound.

I take off my cardigan. I put it back on. I can't get settled.

Where does Shelley go at night?

I put my hand in the pocket of my cardigan. I feel something—a piece of a paper.

I take it out and look at it. It's one of the handwritten notes from my apartment.

Horizontal transfers of genes.

Pursuit of life at all costs.

The worst fever I had was when I was twelve. I was in bed for a week. The doctor told my parents that I was seriously ill, that it was touch and go. My temperature was 102. I couldn't keep anything down.

This fever is worse.

I feel like I've been hit by a train, dragged for a few miles, and dropped in a ditch.

I can't focus. I can't stop shaking from cold, but the sweat pours off me. There are people around my bed, coming in and out of my room. Are they packing? Jack? Is that Jack?

Shelley?

Two people are talking at the foot of my bed. I can hear Pete's violin.

Someone is walking me to the bathroom. They hold my forehead. I'm vomiting.

It's night, then day, then night, then day again.

I'm so thirsty.

I yell for a drink, but now, just when I need it, no one's here. I'm alone again. *Help me.* It's dark. I'm shivering, but I need water. I make myself get out of bed, and on shaky legs, I walk slowly to the bathroom to get a drink.

It's so dark that I have to feel for the bathroom light switch with my hand, running it up and down the wall. It shouldn't take this long. Where is it? I find it and flip it up. The light comes on, and I scream.

But I don't make a sound. I just feel myself scream. I can feel it inside my body.

What is he doing here? In front of me. Sitting in my chair. He has a canvas in his lap. He's working on it intensely, painting. He hates being interrupted when he's working. I can't believe he's here. He looks so old. I saw him the day he died, and he didn't look this old. He looks up from his work. Right at me.

"What? What is it now? What the hell do you want? Can't you see I'm working? Leave me alone! I need time. There's more to do."

I stumble back, dizzy, flipping the light off, as I fall back into bed, shaking, and crawl under the covers.

Part Three

"Good morning."

I open my eyes to a blur of shapeless color. I try to focus.

Jack is standing at my bedside. My head feels heavy, and I'm not sure where I am. Then I remember: A fever, Jack, the kitchen. Seeing him in that frantic state. I couldn't speak. He was crying. I saw his tears.

Was that part of my dream? I was so sick. For how long? Days? A week? I have no idea.

But what I do recall, vividly, is seeing *him*. I saw him last night. He was here. He was sitting in my chair, painting.

I look at Jack, who seems rested and fresh, not the way he appeared in the darkness of the kitchen.

"What happened?" I ask, my voice broken and hoarse.

"You were sick," he says. "An upset tummy."

"Since when?"

"Since dinner last night. Something didn't agree with you. I was here all night, helping you. How are you feeling now?"

"You were with me here? Last night?" I say.

He nods.

I sit up. I feel old but . . . okay. I feel like myself again. I feel like I did yesterday, before it all happened. The bed is still soft, warm. Jack is looking after me.

"That was rough," I say. "I feel like I was sick for a week."

"Food poisoning is brutal. You were running a high fever."

I take a sip of water from the glass by my bed. It's cold and soothes my scratchy throat.

"Did anyone else get sick?" I ask, putting my hand to my head.

"Yes, everyone," he says.

"What about you and Shelley?"

———

"How do you feel now?" he asks. "Any appetite yet?"

I consider eating a plate of eggs and toast, and, shockingly, my stomach grumbles.

"Yes," I say. "Actually, I'm hungry."

"That's a good sign."

Jack hands me a smooth device that easily fits in my hand.

"I brought you something," he whispers, leaning down. "But don't tell the others."

I look at the device in my hands. "What's this?"

"Music," he says. "For your headphones. It's an iPod. I didn't forget."

"I don't know how to use this," I say.

"Here, I'll show you, it's intuitive," he says.

He takes a moment to show me how to use the device. It does seem like something I'll be able to use.

When he turns to go, I call out to him when he's at the door.

"Why did you do this for me?"

"Because I like you. I like how you talk to me about things. How open you are."

He's about to leave.

"Jack, what happened? When I saw you. You were crying. Are you okay?"

"Everything's okay, Penny. It's a new day. Breakfast is ready whenever you are."

After he leaves, I don't move for a minute or two. I stay lying in bed, trying to steady my thoughts. I feel the top and bottom sheets. They're dry, not soaked in sweat. Did my night of sickness happen yesterday? Right now, this morning, it feels so much longer than that. My head is still foggy, but my tummy rumbles again, telling me it's time for breakfast. I'm already so hungry. I swing my legs out of bed, stand up.

Before putting on my slippers I notice that my toenails are long. My wonky knee isn't as sore as usual. I rub my hand over it and move my leg up and down. It doesn't even feel stiff.

The effects of last night's illness are totally gone. It feels good to feel good. I never said that at my apartment. I never thought that. And I was so sick last night. I feel so much better this morning. Better than ever. The sunlight is filling my room, and it accentuates how blank my walls are. I wish they were decorated. The walls of my apartment were so cluttered and full of photos, posters, paintings.

I also miss my photo albums. I must have had six or seven, all of them full. I used to take them out periodically, flip through them. I loved seeing the old faces.

What happened to all those albums? They aren't here.

I have a hard time remembering the day or two leading up to the move. Mike did all the packing. Did he take everything off the walls? I do remember saying I wanted the photo albums. But why would he pack my paintings instead? What happened to all the stuff I don't miss but used every day: cutlery, glassware, plates? My bed? My kitchen table? My chair? I spent so many hours in that chair.

I realize I'm still holding the small device that Jack left me. I pick up the headphones from the bedside and slip them on. I press play, and immediately my ears are filled with music. Duke Ellington.

I look out the window at the trees. I look at the blank walls. I look up at the ceiling, which is white, like the walls. It's like I'm starting over. A clean slate for however long I have left.

I take off my slippers and start sliding around the room in my bare feet, moving in a way I'm surprised that I still can, in a way I haven't moved in a long time.

I can't believe it. I'm dancing.

It's Shelley, not Jack, serving the breakfast today. That's a first. I feel like I haven't seen her in a while. She doesn't ask me how I'm feeling or offer any sympathy for my night of sickness. There's an intensity to her demeanor this morning, a curtness.

I'm ravenous. I start with a piece of toast. It's already been buttered, but I add more, spreading it right around all the edges so the piece is glistening. We also have fruit and yogurt and hard-boiled eggs. I take two eggs from the platter.

We eat. We all feed attentively; such a basic human need.

I look up from my plate, toward Hilbert. I would guess he's older than me. But I'm not interested in how many years old he his. There are other ways to gauge time and experience.

"How long have you been here?" I ask. "At Six Cedars?"

"I don't know," he says. His eyes look different this morning. Not quite as bright and sharp as they were yesterday.

He sprinkles some salt and pepper onto his egg.

"Were you unwell last night? I was very sick," I say.

"You were unwell? Last night? I'm sorry to hear that. I hope you get used to it."

"Used to it?"

"To the days blending in to one another," he says, biting into his egg. "That's what happens here."

Ruth and Pete are busy eating. Pete, as usual, is slumped and focused entirely on his food. I can tell that Ruth is keeping an eye on us, though.

"I'm feeling good here," I whisper. "But I'm still new. I'm still getting used to it."

"This. Each day," he says. "What we do here doesn't change. We work."

Something shifts inside me when he says this.

"We all have our own work, but the days feel the same for us. Space and time are misleading. Think about equivalent fractions. The fractions that have distinct numerators and denominators but are equal to the same value. Three-sixths and four-eighths are both equal to one-half. They're all the same."

He puts the other half of the egg in his mouth.

"Maybe there's something we could do to change that," I say. "So things don't blend together."

"I doubt it. I think it's always been this way here," he says. "I think that's how she wants it."

I take a bite of toast. Chew, swallow.

"Would you sit for me?" I ask.

It takes him a few seconds to understand what I've just asked. He wipes his mouth with his napkin and appears to perk up.

"I'm not sure she'd condone that," he says.

"I'm not sure, either," I say.

"Well," he says, making a ticking sound with his tongue as he thinks. "Yes."

The way he answers, it almost sounds like he's asking me a question. But I don't care. He said yes.

The last person to sit for me was a woman from our building. It must have been a decade ago. She wasn't familiar with art or portraiture or surrealism. She was a single mother, a server at a café two streets over. She had the most remarkable face: perfectly round and lined and serene. I wanted her to see her face how I saw it. The beauty, the toughness, the grace, the experience. It was all there. But like all my work, I never felt like my painting of her was finished, so I never showed it to her.

A flare of excitement in my belly, a tingling.

I nod and start back into my breakfast, helping myself to a third egg.

"It's time for a meeting," Shelley says brusquely, as she clears our empty plates away.

We don't say anything, but stand and start toward the common room. I'm trying to catch Hilbert's eye, but he doesn't look my way, as if he believes he's not supposed to. His expression is flat and hard to read as he stares straight ahead.

We walk single file along the hallway. The only sounds are our footsteps and Shelley humming behind us.

We all find our seats. It's warmer in here than in the dining room or in the hallway. I can feel the sun's heat from the window on my arm. No one speaks. Not Hilbert or Ruth. Of course not Pete. Not even Shelley. She's just sitting there, smiling, looking back at us.

What is this? What's going on?

It's so quiet that I bring a hand up to my ear to feel if I'm wearing my noise-canceling headphones, but I'm not.

IAIN REID

Still, no one speaks. Including me. I could say something. I could be the one to talk, to break the ice, but I don't.

It's windier today. I can see it moving the branches of the trees outside. It's pretty. No leaves on the trees, just bare boughs and twigs. They must be so old, the trees. They've been here much longer than this house.

"Jack?" Shelley says, breaking the silence.

I turn from the window, to her. I didn't know Jack was in the hall. Why wasn't he at breakfast? Why is he waiting out there?

"Jack, you can come in now, please."

I'm the only one to turn toward the doorway. Jack walks in but doesn't say anything.

"Closer," she says.

He obeys, stepping closer, walking past me and toward her. Our eyes meet briefly. Shelley rises to her full height. She's several inches taller than he is. The gap between them looks greater than I thought it was. She picks up a chair and carries it into the center of the half circle.

"Have a seat."

Jack, in his white scrubs, hesitates, then sits down nervously, one leg bouncing. I look at Hilbert, Pete, and then Ruth. They're all focused intently on Jack. They look disappointed. It's as if they've all taken on Shelley's disposition.

"You never get to participate in our discussions," she says. "I'm sorry you got left out."

He stares at the ground and clears his throat.

"Why don't you share something with us?"

He's antsy. He can't sit still.

"Like what?" he asks, making eye contact with her. "What do you have in mind?"

"Oh, I don't know. Like what you did before working here."

What did he do to upset her? Why is she confronting him, in front of us, like this? Is it possible she saw him the same way I did? Upset, scared, wretched, drinking wine. Is she trying to make a point?

"I was unemployed," he says.

"Were you living with anyone?"

"No."

I don't like how she's talking to him. It's aggressive. I'm feeling un-comfortable for Jack. For all of us.

"What was your place like?"

"Where I lived?"

"Yes."

"Small."

"Cozy?"

Ruth is about to speak when Shelley holds up her hand. "Just let Jack speak for now, Ruth."

"No," he says. "It was a crappy place."

Shelley stands and walks toward the window. She stands there in the sun, looking out at the forest.

"Do you like it here? With us?"

"Yes."

"What do you like about it?"

"I get to work and live and be part of the group."

"You get to work here. Earn a real living. It's a privilege. Everyone needs a purpose. Our work fulfills us."

"I'm lucky to have this job," he says.

Shelley turns back with a bright grin on her face. Her eyes are glowing. I've never seen her smile so widely.

"I'm so happy you feel that way. And we feel lucky to have you."

Jack stands. Without looking at Shelley, or any of us, he rushes out. I'm in shock.

Once he's gone, Ruth stands up.

"Jack is still one of us, right?" she asks Shelley.

"Of course he's one of us," she says. "We all need a little encouragement from time to time. That's all. To remember where our priorities lie and what's most important."

What was that? What just happened?

Was Shelley mad at Jack?

Was she trying to embarrass him? Make a point that she's the boss, that she's always in control, that he needs this job, that he can be replaced, that he doesn't have anything without us, without this house?

I don't know Shelley. Not at all. I live with her. She bathes me and washes my hair. She looks after us. But it takes time to get to know someone, to understand their motivations and beliefs.

I keep replaying what she said to Jack in my mind. I'm sitting in my chair, in my room, my bed to the right, when all of a sudden it dawns on me: this isn't my room. It's someone else's.

I came straight here after the meeting. I walked in alone, used the washroom, sat down, and am only now understanding my mistake.

This must be Ruth's room.

What a stupid mistake to make. How foolish I am.

I wonder what Ruth would think if she saw me in here like this, sitting in her chair. She wouldn't like it. She would be very upset. The room looks almost identical to mine. The most obvious difference is that she has a French-English dictionary on her desk where I have my tin of brushes.

I know I shouldn't, but I can't resist. I'll be quick. I sit down on her bed. It's soft and supportive like my own. I can't tell the difference. I lean back, roll over onto my side, and smell the duvet.

I stand and walk over to her dresser. Instead of a framed photo and sculpture, she has a small glass bottle. I pick it up. I open the lid and smell it. I recognize the scent immediately. It's a perfume I used to love. I had the same kind. I only ever bought it once, and I wore it sparingly. The bottle lasted me for years and years.

I remember he never liked it. That's the reason I stopped wearing it. I'm sure it was this one.

He never specifically said to get rid of it, but I knew not to wear it around the apartment when he was home. It wasn't worth it for the comments I'd get. I'd only wear it when I was going out without him. He would get very dramatic about it. I can see his eyes, his slumped shoulders, the way he'd sigh, his exasperated expression as if my wearing perfume was somehow an affront to him.

I take another sniff. The scent hasn't changed over all these years. It's uncanny.

As I take a long inhale of the perfume, I remember. I remember us talking about this place, Six Cedars. We did discuss it. We talked about how beautiful the house looked. How nice it would be to live so close to a big forest. That I'd always wanted to live somewhere near a forest. I'd completely forgotten this until right now. I wanted to live here.

I take another sniff.

I listen to make sure no one is coming down the hall. I dab some on my finger, behind my ear, my wrist. I rub my wrists together. I can't help myself. I replace the lid, set the perfume back down, and walk out to find Hilbert.

"**D**id you know that *n* is the mathematical reference for an uncertain number?" says Hilbert.

"No," I say.

"Such a small thing, just a letter, but it is necessary."

"You have such a different way of seeing things from my way," I say.

"That's how I feel about you," he says.

"There are things that you understand that I don't."

"And vice versa," he says. "After we talk, I keep thinking about the things you tell me," he says.

I feel a warmth spread across my chest.

"How many days have we known each other?"

"I'm not sure. Does the sum matter?"

"I was wondering if we might try something," I say.

"When?" he asks.

"Today," I say. "Now."

"Right now?"

"Yes."

"What do you want to try?"

"I want to keep it a secret. Just between us."

"Okay, Penny," he says.

"Come with me," I say, reaching out and taking hold of his long, heavy hand.

We shuffle along the hallway in our slippers, hand in hand, to my room. Just us. We can be alone in here. It's quiet. I ask him to sit in the chair while I prepare my paint. He's fidgeting with the cuff of his jacket.

"You can relax," I say.

"I've never done this before," he says.

"That's a good thing."

As I prep, I glance at Hilbert, how he sits, the slight tremble in his hands, how he's peering around the room. He's still curious at this age, still thoughtful.

"Were you married, Hilbert? Before you came here?"

"I was married. I'm a widower."

"I'm sorry," I say.

"We had a long time together," he says.

He has settled, and I start painting.

"What was she like?"

"She was smart," he says. "Intensely logical. That was the first thing I loved about her. Were you married?"

"No, but I had a partner for many years. We lived together. He was an artist."

"Did you study how to do that?" he asks.

"Painting?"

"Yes."

"No, not formally, just on my own. Reading books, trying things, going to galleries. I don't like saying 'self-taught' because so much has influenced me."

"That's probably for the best. I studied for a long time, many years, most of my early adulthood—formal, academic study. I never thought I would enjoy teaching, but I did."

"You taught math at university?"

"Yes, and had my own work to keep me busy. There was pressure to publish. I felt that pressure less and less as I got older but kept working. I've filled lots of blue graph paper over the years."

"It's like you came back to what got you started in the first place."

"It was my mom who got me started. She taught me basic arithmetic at our kitchen table."

I can picture him as a young man, actually see him that way, sitting hunched over a desk, holding his pencil.

"That's so nice. And that's what hooked you?"

"I suppose so," he says. "I never stopped after that. There was always more to learn."

"Yes, I feel the same, but for different reasons. Painting always felt like a playground, for emotion. Not just my own. It was about borders, physical borders. It always felt like the art I liked found me, not the other way around."

"Yes, yes, I see. I know what you mean," he says.

He's holding his position remarkably well, sitting back in the chair, shoulders straight.

"The one thing I regret about never showing my own work is missing the chance for that process where another person reacts in their own distinct way. It's not about understanding it, it's about having a reaction. Any reaction."

"So you've never shown your work? You never had an opening?"

"No," I say. "I never have."

He uncrosses his legs and looks at me directly. I can tell he's wondering if that's okay, to break the pose. I nod.

"You don't have to stay in one position," I say. "Whatever's comfortable."

He exhales, lets his shoulders slump slightly, and shifts how he's sitting.

"Are you aware of the Riemann hypothesis?"

"No," I say. "What's that?"

"We'd have to start with prime numbers and go back to Euclid, who was first to prove that there are infinitely many primes. Infinitely many! The Riemann itself has never been proved but . . ." He stops himself, trailing off. "That's funny, I'm just trying to get it straight."

He takes a moment to think.

"I used to know all of this by heart and how to describe it. I'm afraid it's just not coming right now. I'm sorry."

He looks down, blushing.

"It's okay. I thought that I completely understood the point of painting, but as I got older I started thinking that art is about different ways of seeing. I was never inspired by something whole. It was always a fragment, a crumb, a piece of a moment, a half-forgotten impression, one side of a person. Never fully formed because it could only be my view of a thing, not someone else's."

"Like me, right now?"

"Yes. Like you. Right now."

He smiles, runs his fingers through his white hair. "Everything changes," he says.

"Even just in the last few days, I feel like I've changed. I know I have. Drastically. I'm eating more, sleeping better. Meeting you has changed me, too," I say.

"We're taken care of here. So we can just live."

For a while I paint in quiet.

"It felt so comfortable when I first arrived," I say. "But something is worrying me."

"About here?"

"Yes. Has she ever talked to Jack like that before?"

"Shelley?"

"Yes. She humiliated him in front of us. It was strange."

"I'm . . . sorry," he says, looking perplexed. "I don't remember if she has done that kind of thing before."

"That's okay. It doesn't matter."

"My mind certainly isn't as sharp as it used to be. My memory seems to come and go."

"Yes," I say. "Mine, too. Certain things just fade."

"I suppose living as we do, it makes the current moment the most important. Each one, until the next."

"Does it scare you?" I ask.

"What?"

"Living moment to moment. Not being able to remember."

"Yes," he says. "It does."

"Me, too," I say.

I pause my work as Hilbert coughs into his hand and then clears a dry spot from his throat.

"But maybe that's not a bad thing," he says. "Being scared."

"I really appreciate this," I say. "Having you in here."

"I was happy you asked me to sit for you. I'm nervous to go through with it but tickled you asked."

"I've never talked about my memory with anyone else."

"At least not that you can remember," he says, smiling.

I've never been able to examine him so closely, so intently. His face, hands. His eyes. The dimple on his chin.

"We should keep helping each other when we can," I say.

"Look out for each other," he says.

"The more we talk together," I say.

"The more we understand," he adds, finishing my sentence.

A door closes down the hall. I pause, waiting to hear footsteps, but there aren't any. Just quiet.

"Us talking together, even if we're not going anywhere, is our own little uprising," I say.

"Our private revolt," he says, and we both laugh.

After some time, I stop, set my brush down.

"I was thinking maybe . . ."

"What?"

"No, it's silly."

He gives me an encouraging look.

"Maybe," I say, "you could take off your shirt?"

I hadn't planned to ask this. The idea hadn't come into my mind until right now. This moment. He doesn't say anything. His expression is ambiguous. I shouldn't have suggested it.

"No," he says, after a long pause. "I don't think you want to see an old man with his shirt off."

"I do. A body is more fascinating with age. It's more honest."

To my surprise, he nods.

I stand up, walk over to him until I'm about a foot away. I start to untie his tie, but I fumble with the knot before I'm able to slide it off. I remove his jacket. I start at the top, slowly unbuttoning his shirt, my hands becoming steady again. I feel my cheeks growing warm as I get to the last button. I see the same reddening of Hilbert's cheeks.

"I can feel my heart beating," he says.

He takes my hand and puts it on his bare chest. His skin is hairless and soft. I can feel he's perspiring, just a bit.

"Thank you," he says.

"Thank you," I say.

I feel my own heat, my own heart beating, the way Hilbert's is.

"Would you mind standing?" I ask.

He does, and for a moment we just look at each other. We take each other in. His skin is wrinkled and droops. An old man's imperfect torso. Years on display in that sagging skin: quiet moments of pride and shame, excitement and fear, joy, guilt, desire, happiness, loss, love. I can see it. All of it and more. Just like my own.

We don't say anything else as I continue my work.

can't say for how long he stands there like that, shoulders straight, hands at his side, shirt off. His eyes fixed on the floor, or out the window. Certain moments he looks deep in thought, at others he cracks a smile for no apparent reason. It's impressive that he can stand for so long. It must be an hour. Maybe more.

At one point he says to me: "$7 \div \frac{2}{3} = 7 \times 3/2$. If dividing by a fraction, you can reverse the fraction and multiply."

I ask if he's tired, if he's cold, if he wants a break. Each time, he says no. He says I should just keep going.

I do. I keep painting, losing myself in the work. I've been adding details to his chin and lips until I feel a shift in the room. I hadn't noticed it before, but now it's unmistakable—the feeling that someone else is here with us. Another presence.

"We should take a break," I say.

I slip my cardigan over my shoulders and help Hilbert with his shirt.

"What's that?" I ask, noticing something, a bump, on the back of his neck.

I reach across his shoulder to touch it with my finger. What is it? A mole? A pimple? It looks like some kind of strange growth, like a cluster of tiny mushrooms. He flinches when I touch it.

Shelley walks in without knocking. She looks at us, standing together, Hilbert's shirt half-unbuttoned, my hand on his neck. I have an urge to hide my brush, the paint. I want to cover the portrait. This was supposed to be our secret. From her. From the others.

"What are you doing in here?" she asks Hilbert. "I've been looking for him. It's time for his nap."

"Already? What time is it?"

She ignores me.

"Come on, Hilbert. Let's go."

"But he has some marks," I say. "On his neck. Raised bumps."

This stops her in her tracks.

"Marks?" she says.

"Yes, they look sore."

Hilbert reaches up and touches the spot on his neck.

"That's enough now, Penny. Don't upset Hilbert."

"I'm not upsetting him."

"Yes, you are. You have an overactive imagination, which is good for your work, but I don't want that to get the better of you."

Hilbert leans in to me, speaking softly, so Shelley won't hear.

"I want you to paint marks on me if that's what you see," he whispers. "Paint what you see."

"Come," Shelley says, and she ushers him out.

It's not until they're gone that I realize I can hear Pete playing his violin.

Now it's just me. Single. Solitary. Unattended. A hermit. Alone in my room, just like being back in my apartment. No Hilbert. No one to talk to. No one to touch. No one to paint.

I walk into my bathroom, run the warm water, and splash some on my face, neck, and on my wrists.

What did I just see on Hilbert's skin? Was it there when I was painting? If it was, I didn't notice. Maybe I'm imagining it. Perhaps it was only a shadow. We can't always trust our senses.

I slowly turn in a full circle, looking at the walls of my room, then down at my arms and hands. I have a strong instinct to crawl into my bed and get under the blanket, to lock my door. I play around with the door handle.

There is no lock on my door. I can't lock my door.

I go into my bathroom again and check the door and frame. No lock here, either. I inspect the area around the sink and mirror. I open the shower curtain. I walk back out into the room and over to the window, the fading daylight.

I haven't been outside since I've arrived here. Not once. I want to breathe the fresh air, feel it on my face.

It's been too long. We're all breathing the same air in here. I used to go outside, walk to the park, sit on the bench near the path. Fresh air is essential to humans, to animals, to plants and trees.

I walk to my desk and bedside table, flipping on the lamp, flipping it back off. On. Off. On. Off. The click settles me. Hilbert's unfinished portrait gazes back at me.

I sit down on my bed. In the quiet. I hear a faint buzzing, almost like an insect, a bee. I tilt my head, trying to hear better. It's almost indistinguishable from the silence.

I get up again, walk back to my desk. The sound is louder the closer I get to it, until I'm standing right at the desk. Above me is a light bulb. Just like at my apartment. When I fell. I hit my head. Someone was inside the apartment with me. I woke up with blood on my head, blood on the floor.

I turn the chair around, and with some difficulty, am able to get one knee up on the chair, then the other. From the chair I step up onto the desk. My old joints work. I didn't fall this time. My room looks different from up here, smaller. I steady myself and then, using the wall for leverage, I go up on my tiptoes, getting as close to the light as possible. The light is definitely the source of the buzzing sound. I'm so close. I close my eyes . . . listening.

Little, old honeybees . . . they're actually smart enough to engage in mathematics.

Who said that? Who told me that? When did I hear that?

I open my eyes.

I'm standing on my desk. I look around my room. I'm alone. I can still hear the buzzing, but it's no longer an indecipherable droning. It's familiar. Voices. People talking all at once. Voices over one another. None of it is clear. I'm trying desperately to understand what they're saying.

I close my eyes.

I see faces. The faces of the others. Of us. It's us. Pete, Ruth, Hilbert. I can see them close up, each face, lips and teeth, biting food, chewing, swallowing, eating. Pete, Ruth, Hilbert. Pete with his violin. Ruth conjugating French verbs. Hilbert leaning over his graph paper, pencil in hand.

Pete, Ruth, Hilbert. Hideously old. Grotesque. Repulsive to be so old. Despicable. All of us, walking together in a circle, for our own protection.

It's completely dark outside my window. How long have I been standing here atop my desk? My feet are sore.

I bring my hand up, and with my arm fully extended, I touch the light with the tip of my index finger.

I scream, pulling it back immediately, almost falling off the desk.

The light has burned my finger. I climb back down. My feet are firmly on the floor. I hold my burnt finger with my other hand. Squeezing it. I pace back and forth. Jack must have heard my scream. He rushes into my room.

"What's wrong, Penny? Are you okay?"

I look at him. He wants to help me. But I can't bring myself to tell him the truth about what has happened. He might be mad at me. He might tell Shelley I was standing on my desk.

"I hurt my finger," I say.

"Oh no. Let me see. What happened?"

"I . . . caught it in the door."

He looks at the finger, sees that it's red. Then, he looks me right in the eye.

"Does it still hurt?"

"It's fine. I'm fine."

"It was your room door you caught it in?"

"Yes," I lie.

He looks at me, as if he knows it's not true. It's the first time I've lied to him.

"There are no locks on my door," I say.

"What?"

"Why can't I lock my door?"

"Don't you remember? We explained that. Here," he says. "Have a seat."

He helps me down into my desk chair.

"I only noticed today, before I hurt my finger."

"The locks were removed as part of the renovation," Jack says.

Light bulbs shouldn't buzz like that. Or be so hot. Doors should have locks.

"People need privacy," I say.

"People here need help. She doesn't like the idea of locks. Not here."

"Why?"

Jack glances behind him, toward the hall, then back to me.

"For many reasons, Penny," he says irritably. "Locks can be dangerous in a place like this."

"A place like this?"

"Where the residents have certain . . . struggles. Where memory is an issue."

"My memory is fine," I say.

He rubs his forehead with his hands, then his eyes.

"There's lots of confusion here. Locks would be a bad idea."

"Not even my bathroom door has a lock!"

"No one's going to bother you while you're in there."

"How do I know that?"

Jack steps closer.

"Do you forget you had a fall when you climbed up onto your desk?"

"Desk? I fell from a chair. In my apartment. In my kitchen."

I feel myself instinctively bring a hand up to my forehead, where the scab is. I don't feel anything. I run my hand all over my forehead. No scab. No scar. Nothing. Just dry, wrinkled skin. That can't be. The scar was still there yesterday. I've been here only a few days.

"Is there something I don't know about, Jack?"

"What do you mean?"

"Here. Her. This house."

He smiles, puts a hand on my shoulder.

"You're fitting in so well."

"I'm talking about a feeling. It's been growing." Something's wrong in this house. In my room."

"I don't know what you mean."

"Are you watching me?"

Jack rolls his eyes, shakes his head. "Penny, come on. We have to know what's going on around here. To make sure everyone's safe."

I can hear the faint buzzing again, from high up. I try to peer up at the light without letting him see. I don't want him to know what I'm looking at.

"So, there's nothing I don't know about, in my room? I don't feel like myself. I feel something is . . . here with me, and I don't like it."

In me. Inside me. I don't say it, but it feels like it's expanding, growing, connecting us, binding us forever. "Why are there only four of us living here?" I ask. "Only four residents?"

0.1666666666

"Because we're a small residence. It's good to be curious, Penny. But we don't want curiosity to become paranoia."

"I'm not paranoid!"

"Didn't you think you were being watched at your old place, too?"

I think back to my days at the apartment. The person standing on the street, staring up at me. The voices next door. The man who came to fix my outlets. Mike, checking on me, packing, bringing me here.

"There was someone on the street," I say.

Jack bends down, leaning over me. "And you say they were watching you? They never said anything, never tried to approach you, or hurt you?"

"They never talked to me, no. But I believe they knew that I was alone. And they were watching me. It could have been her."

Observing me, selecting me, preying on me because I'm old and alone. Maybe I didn't pick this place. Maybe I was picked. Selected. Now that I'm here, she has each day planned for us. Meals and naps. She decides when we wake up and when we go to bed. There's no one to check up on me, visit, or ask how I'm doing here. She would know that.

"I know it was a tough time for you before you got here," he says. "But I need you to remember that the mind can play tricks on us.

This old house is here to keep you all safe and comfortable. That's all."

"I may not remember everything," I say. "But my mind is fine."

I can tell he's getting antsy by the way he's holding his hands, rubbing his fingers. He sighs in frustration.

"Penny, a lesson I've learned while working here is that we're not always aware of change as it's happening. Most change happens gradually, not overnight. You have nothing to worry about."

He turns to go, walking to the door.

"For a while, when I was younger," I say, which stops him, "I thought I would paint more."

He's right at the door with his back toward me, but he's listening.

"I honestly believed that at some point I'd get over my insecurities and people would see my pictures. I thought that's why I painted, you know, so eventually people could see my work, be moved or disturbed, so people would react to it. I thought that was the point."

He doesn't turn. He doesn't move.

"I've been hearing things," I say.

Now he looks at me.

"That's why I gave you those headphones."

"But why am I hearing noises I've never heard before?"

"Because you were alone before."

"And now?" I ask.

"And now we live here together. The headphones will help. That's exactly what they're for. You'll be able to focus and paint for as long as you want."

"Those headphones will help with how I feel?"

"They'll help with the sounds you're hearing. It's an old house. Thin walls. It took you a long time to get used to the creaky floors, too, Penny."

A long time? I just got here.

"Call me if you need anything else," he says.

should listen to Jack. Jack has been good to me. He likes me. I can trust him.

I try on my headphones, without any music this time. When I slip them over my ears, there's no sound at all. Again, I feel the sensation of being underwater, submerged.

I stand and walk around my room, but I can't even hear my own steps. I move over to my desk. I pick up my dry brush. I pretend to paint, mimicking the movements, as if I'm adding to the portrait of Hilbert, making subtle progress.

I look at myself in the mirror. I turn to the side, examine my profile, my posture. I stand as straight as Ruth.

"Bonjour," I say with my bad French accent.

I think I've actually lost a few pounds. I can't believe it considering how much I'm eating. Physically, I feel unimpaired, almost robust.

But what I notice most today are my eyes. They are hazy, hollow, the color dimmer. It's not drastic. It's subtle. But they remind me of Pete's eyes.

No one else would even notice. But I do.

Another day. Another meal. More food. Ruth is talking up a storm, as usual. She's rattling on about two or three things at once. She's doing enough talking for all of us. She's become predictable. How she speaks and throws her head back when she laughs.

Hilbert came and sat for me again, not long after I woke up. It was his idea this time. He sat near the window, looking tired but handsome in the morning light.

I've noticed Hilbert has been speaking less the last couple of meals. Not to the same completely nonverbal extent as Pete, but even his eyes look more distant. It's sad. He eats with the same vigor, though, as we all do. I'm worried about him.

Ruth is laughing at her own joke. A big belly laugh. Uproarious.

The entire day goes by in a blink of an eye. We sleep at the same time. We have our meetings. We nap. We have free time to work on whatever we want. Morning to afternoon to evening. It's only strange when I think about it after the fact. Not when we're in it. In the moment we're just living, consuming, occupying, sustaining, going forward, from one thing to the next. I was painting a lot today. Focused, engrossed in the picture. I'm trying to catch Hilbert's eye, but he's focused on eating.

Cutting, biting, chewing, swallowing.

"How is it Hilbert?" I ask.

He nods and offers a sound of mellow satisfaction. But he doesn't stop eating. He doesn't engage the way I expect him to. The way I want him to.

We're all so captivated by our food. We eat fiendishly. It's not about enjoyment but sustenance, just getting as much as possible. Do we really need to eat so much? I scan down and see that I, too, have already finished half of my plate. I stab a piece of carrot with my fork. I'm still hungry, but I don't put the piece in my mouth. I pretend to. I check to confirm that Jack isn't watching, and slip the carrot into my napkin while I imitate chewing and swallowing. No one is paying me any attention. I do it again, with another piece of carrot.

Then I glance up to see that Ruth, still babbling away, is looking right at me.

She must have seen what I did with the carrots, but she doesn't say anything. She just turns back to her own food. Before she eats another bite, though, Ruth starts laughing. It's a quiet laugh at first, muffled. But she continues, and it gets louder.

"Stop that, please. We can't eat with all that," Hilbert says. He sets his cutlery down, refusing to eat until Ruth stops.

He looks older to me. Frail. As if he's aged overnight.

"You look tired. I think you should rest," I say to Hilbert, but I don't think he hears me.

Ruth is still laughing.

"It's not funny," I say to Ruth.

Jack steps over to calm Hilbert. Shelley appears from the kitchen and walks over to Ruth.

"That's enough now, Ruth," Shelley says.

Ruth puts one hand over her mouth but then starts laughing again. Louder this time.

Shelley turns to me. "Are you all done, Penny?"

"Yes, I am."

Jack starts to clear some of the plates.

"We didn't get it all," Ruth says. "Two little pieces of carrot."

I feel myself shiver.

Ruth sticks her tongue out at me.

"Ruth, leave Penny alone," says Shelley. "Jack, will you help Ruth back to her room?"

I stare at the spot on the table where my plate was. Jack helps Ruth up from her chair. I can feel her eyes on me. Her arm brushes by mine as she leaves the table.

"What are you doing to Hilbert? What have you done to him?" I ask Shelley.

But she's gone back to the kitchen and doesn't hear me.

"Come on, Ruth," Jack calls from the door. "Let's go."

I don't look up again until Shelley sets a teacup down in front of me.

"I think I'd prefer to go back to my room now," I say. "If that's okay."

"What about your tea and dessert? You never miss those."

"No, I don't need anything else right now."

"You don't want to miss your dessert. You love cherry pie."

"I'd rather take it back to my room. I'm tired."

"Well, we don't usually eat in the rooms, but it's not a strict rule. I'll carry it for you."

Shelley, a couple of paces behind, carrying the tea in one hand and the dessert in the other, follows me back to my room. I enter my room first and sit down in my reading chair. It groans under my weight as I sink into it. Shelley puts the food down on top of the dresser.

"It's here for whenever you're ready for it. But best not to let it sit too long."

She's about to go when she takes a moment to look around the room. I've hidden the portrait between my desk and the wall. I feel terribly self-conscious about it. I'm embarrassed I don't have more done. I should be further along. I'm hoping she doesn't notice.

Shelley steps toward me.

I bring my hands together in my lap, curling my fingers to cover my nails. She bends down and gently takes hold of my left hand.

"Oh, look at this," she says, running her thumb across each of my nails. She checks my other hand. "They're getting a bit jagged. We'll have to fix you up."

Shelley continues rubbing my hand for a moment longer than feels normal.

"Does it matter?"

"Pardon?" she says.

"Does it matter if my nails get jagged or long or if I bite them? Why are you obsessed with my nails?"

"I'm obsessed with taking care of you, Penny, and your nails don't stop growing."

Shelley lets go of my hand. It drops into my lap. I hear her footsteps all the way down the hall, until my room is silent. I get up, standing in front of the window. I put my ear to the cool glass. I can't hear anything out there. Nothing.

I button my cardigan, shuffle out of the room in my slippers. I walk along the hallway, past the seats in the cove, to the common room. I poke my head in and see the chairs in the semicircle. No one's here. I step in and go to the shelf of books and games. I pick up two boxes of puzzles amid a collection of board games.

Carrying the puzzles under my arm, I walk to Hilbert's room. I need to see him, find out how he's doing. I knock on his door, and when he doesn't answer, I go in. He's getting ready for bed, and it's not until I'm inside that I hear him, whistling quietly to himself. He turns around, surprised to see me, his eyes brightening.

"Sorry," I say. "I'm not tired . . . I thought maybe . . ."

"Hello," he says cheerfully.

I want to ask him if Shelley is as concerned about his nails as she is about mine. I want to ask him if he feels pressure to keep going, to keep working. I want to see if those marks, that fungus, is still there.

There's so much to say, to ask, but more than anything, I just want to see him.

"Thank you again for sitting for me," I say.

Hilbert doesn't reply. But he tilts his head as if trying to remember.

"How about a quick diversion before bed?" I ask. "I know how much you love puzzles."

let him choose. The box he picks reads "Pando Puzzle" on the front and has a nature scene, a large forest. Hilbert shakes all the pieces out on the desk. It's not until I pick up the empty box that I see how similar it is to this place, to the scenery right here, outside the house. It's striking. Still holding the box, I walk to the window, holding it up.

"Look," I say. "It's almost the same."

Hilbert's already focused on the puzzle, picking up pieces, trying to find matches.

"Isn't that strange," I say.

Hilbert looks at me. "All those trees out there look just like these," he says. "I've looked at them a long time. There are so many, but they end up blending together."

I stare out at them. I try not to blink. He's right.

"Have we done this one before?" he asks. "You and I?"

"I don't think so," I say.

"We should take turns," he says. "With the pieces."

I lean against the desk, and we put the pieces together one at a time, as we find them, occasionally glancing up at each other.

I feel my stomach grumble. When was dinner? When did we last eat?

"I believe," he says, "that Pando is the world's biggest organism. And certainly one of the oldest."

Hilbert fits one piece with another. Then I do the same.

"It," he says.

"What?" I ask.

"It. The trees. The Pando. There are many trees, but they're actually one . . . all together."

"What do you mean?"

I join two more pieces of the firm cardboard.

"It's a colony. A colony that began from a single tree."

"Isn't it a forest?"

Hilbert finds two pieces he likes and tries fitting them together.

"They, each one, share the same genetic markers. It's a single root system."

"What does that mean?"

He's trying to force them. They clearly don't fit.

"It's okay," I say. "Here."

I take one of the pieces from him and offer an alternative. He slips it in place, then looks up at me.

"They're all connected by their root system," he says. "I think she has plans for us."

"Shelley?"

I reach over and touch his leg. He rests his hand on mine, squeezing it softly.

Hilbert didn't want to finish the puzzle. Neither did I. He wasn't feeling well. He wanted to go to bed, so we said good night, and I left him to sleep. I'm back in my room, but I don't feel like crawling into bed. Was it only two nights ago that I saw Jack in the kitchen, that I felt so terribly sick? I look at the framed photo on my dresser, facing away from me, toward the window. I didn't want to feel him looking at me.

All of a sudden, a metallic taste fills my mouth. I look down and see I'm biting my thumbnail. I remove it from my mouth.

My nails are very long. On both my hands. The tips curl up above my fingers. How can they grow so fast? I just had them clipped for . . . the party. When is the party?

How long does it take nails to grow? I remember having to cut his nails the last few weeks, when he was too weak to do it. He said he thought his nails and hair might grow for a while after he died. But I told him that wasn't true. In death, the skin retracts, which makes it look like the hair and nails are growing when they're not.

I look at the piece of pie and cup of tea sitting on my desk from dinner. I bring a hand up to my ear and feel the noise-canceling headphones. When did I put these on? I wasn't wearing them in Hilbert's room. There's no noise at all. No music. Only a deep, booming silence.

I inspect the food sitting on my dresser, sniffing it, eyeing it closely. I pick up the fork and use it to cut off a piece of the pie. The texture of the pie has changed. I mash it with the fork. It has taken on the consistency of melted cheese. I drop the fork on the floor.

I try to steady my hand, touching the piece of pie with my finger, pushing it in. I lift my finger as high as I can, and a thin strand of the pie stays connected to the fork. It feels like melted mozzarella, like the cheese I used to grate over my lasagna.

I'm scared to look into the teacup. I peer in as I swirl the cup around. The brown liquid is much thicker than tea should be. It's almost more like a dark pudding. Horrified, I drop the cup on the dresser, where it tips and spills.

I don't clean it up. I don't want to touch it. I start scratching my arm. It feels good with such long nails. I scratch harder and keep going until it tingles and burns. I keep scratching, stepping closer to the mirror until I'm only a foot or so away.

The face looking back at me is mine. My skin is less pale, but I look older. I move my shirt sleeve up so I can see the back of my arm. I see a very small mark, similar to the one I saw on Hilbert's neck that day in my room. Was that today? A blemish. It's small enough that I have to lean even closer. There's still no sound at all. It might just be a pimple.

I move my sleeve up a bit more, to reveal another mark, this one bigger, and protruding from my skin in three dimensions, like fungus, like lichens. Horrified, I lift my shirt more to reveal that almost all of my torso is covered with the bulging fungus.

I look down at my hands. They're shaking. My nails are three times as long as they were a moment ago. As I look again at the mirror, I see my neck and face are covered in the fungus, too.

My head is spinning. I scream.

"Help! Jack!" I yell as loud as I can.

I can't hear myself because of the headphones. I take them off with quivering hands, and as I do, the sound of a violin instantly fills the room. In the mirror I see a small, loose piece of skin near my ear. I move an inch away from the mirror, taking the skin between my fingers, and very slowly pull on it. It starts to peel off, and I keep pulling it until I've peeled it all off. Underneath this skin, it is not my face. It's not my face anymore. It's Ruth.

I'm looking at Ruth's face. Younger, prettier.

There are life-forms of two distinct organisms that flourish as one because of a symbiotic union. I know that's real. I know that happens. I know what Shelley wants.

For us all to keep going, to keep working, to be compatible, to conform and live as one.

I feel my stomach drop. I'm so scared and horrified that I can't help but stumble backward, falling onto my bed.

I wake, coughing, rolling onto my side, the sheet balled up beside me. I'm panting to get a breath. In total darkness, I feel each arm, my stomach, my face. There is no fungus there anymore, only the single, small pimple on the back of my arm.

I rarely have nightmares. It felt so real.

Did Jack help me get into bed? Or was that the night before?

I close my eyes. I focus, but no matter how hard I try, I can't remember going to bed.

What's happening to me?

I sit up, sweaty, disheveled. It's hard to see. The room is so dark. What time is it? The tight feeling in my chest is increasing as if I'm being restrained by an invisible hand. I can feel it in my stomach, too, then my lungs. I slow my breathing by counting to ten. I count to twenty. Then thirty. I feel my heartbeat slow, returning to normal.

That's when I see her. Ruth, standing in the corner of my room, scowling in the shadows, looking at me. She has a hand on her forehead, the same way I do. She's wearing my cardigan.

"Shhhhhhh," she says.

I scream as if I've been doused with boiling water.

"We have to sleep. . . . We have to eat," Ruth says. "Always, always, always. So we can work."

I start to hyperventilate. So does Ruth. She's still standing, but then she positions her body in a hunched fetal position, the same way I'm now lying in bed.

I sit straighter. Ruth stands up straighter, mimicking me exactly.

"What are you doing in here? What do you want? This is my room, not yours. It's not the same."

"It is the same. We have to eat everything we're given," she whispers. "We have to stay warm and rested. So we can keep on going. It's what we want."

I can't help but scream again. Ruth screams with me. After a few moments, Jack runs into the room.

"It's okay," he says. "Calm down. Ruth just got a bit confused."

He walks directly over to her. Like me, she has now stopped yelling, but she's panting. Jack removes my sweater and puts an arm around her. He touches his forehead to hers, softly, whispers something. Immediately, she settles and looks down to the floor.

"Sorry, Penny," Jack says, turning to me. "That must have been a shock. You can go back to sleep."

He speaks to Ruth, reprimanding her, as he walks her out of my room.

It's not right. It's not good. I'm not safe. Not here. This place is bad.

The only thing Shelley cares about is having more time. No matter the cost. The only thing she fears is running out of time. She's keeping us all . . .

Something cracks inside me.

I'm not safe here. None of us are. Was I ever safe? I thought I was. I thought this place was heaven. It felt like it. For a while.

How can I possibly get settled after Ruth's intrusion? I count to a hundred. I count backward from a hundred to zero and back. I walk around my room. I put my chair in front of my door as a blockade.

There's only life here, too much life.

I crawl back into bed, sliding the pillow over my head. I lie still under the blanket. I hear steps from the hall. Doors opening, closing. I hear water running. I hear people talking. I hear laughing, crying. Both. Why is anyone awake right now?

I can't fall asleep.

How long had I been sleeping before Ruth woke me? I still can't remember going to bed. I roll over onto my side. I can't just lie here like this.

I need to move.

I slide on my slippers and tiptoe to the door. I move the chair aside as quietly as possible and open the door.

I take a long time between each step. It feels like minutes. I'm unsteady, and I don't want anyone to hear me. I keep thinking I hear Shelley behind me, or Ruth. But each time I look back, it's only a dark, empty hallway. When the sensor light comes on, I freeze, momentarily, then continue, step by step, toward Hilbert's room.

His door is ajar. I hold on to the frame, peer in. I see his sleeping shape. A human form moving up and down, up and down. Inhale, exhale, inhale, exhale. He's sleeping peacefully. Watching him makes me feel better, safer, more secure. It makes me emotional. I well up.

I look closer. He's wearing his headphones. He's in a deep sleep. It's better not to disturb him. I should let him sleep. I want him to have a rest.

I walk by Pete's room. His door is wide-open. I'm surprised he's not in bed. He is standing in his pajamas, shoulders slumped, with his back to the door. I watch him for a while and see he's holding his violin. He starts playing the same series of notes he always plays. I listen. It never varies. He gets to a certain point, doesn't hit the note he wants, and plays it over, joylessly. Again and again. The same three notes. Over and over and over.

I walk toward the front doors of Six Cedars, to the foyer. As I get closer, my heart starts pounding. Maybe I should seek out Shelley, tell her my suspicions, ask for help to get outside. But I don't even know where she sleeps.

One moment, she'll be right beside me, walking with me through the hallway, helping me sit at dinner, then gone. I won't see her for long stretches of time. This is her house. She's in control here. She can do whatever she wants.

I try to open the front doors, where Mike and I walked in together on the first day, but they're locked. The front door is the only door with locks. The keypad is beside the door with numbers and letters on it. I've never been held against my will before. Never in my life. I've always been able to go outside when I want. To breathe the fresh air and feel the wind. I'm about to push some buttons at random, to see if I can guess the code, to get outside, when I hear Pete's violin echoing down the hall.

Right beside the door, mounted on the wall, is a painting. I used to love this print. Was it always here? *The Little Owl* by Albrecht Dürer. Sixteenth century. Watercolor on paper. The original is in a museum in Vienna, but I've always been captivated by the dark, round eyes of the owl.

I've never wanted to avoid darkness in my own work, my own darkness. But revealing my own shadows is not enough in itself. What I want, what I've always wanted, is for another person to feel relief from their darkness when they look at my work.

The Little Owl doesn't affect me the way it once did. It leaves no mark, no lasting impression. We can't hold on to feelings forever. The violin echoing from Pete's room stirs me from the print.

I look up the staircase. I don't think I've ever been up there. It must be where Shelley goes at night.

Hanging on the wall of the staircase is another framed painting. I have to step up on the first stair to get a good look at it. Like *The Little Owl*, it's another print I recognize from long ago. A famous double portrait from the Italian Renaissance. Oil on wood. Painted by Piero della Francesca. The Duke and Duchess of Montefeltro, both in profile, looking at each other. She died in childbirth, such a short life.

He told me about this portrait one night not long after we'd first met. He explained everything—the context, symbolism, the style, details about the artist. He knew so much about art.

It was around that time he left for Europe for over a month. He asked me to water his plants, which I did. He loved those plants. His studio space was filled with them. I watered them all except for one. It died. I lied and told him I didn't know what had happened to it. I thought he was going to be very upset. He wasn't. He forgot about it within a day.

I don't know why I did it, why I starved his one plant. His not caring about the dead plant made me feel even worse. I spent more time looking after his plants after that, trying to nurture those left. They all lived, continued to grow, but over time I started to wish I hadn't watered any of them. I started to believe that the one I hadn't watered was the lucky one.

I bend down and find a spot on the wall to the left of the staircase, near the bottom, and using a hairpin, I scratch a single mark, one line, into the soft wood.

One mark, for me. If I forget, there will be proof. I'll know that I've been here before.

I open my eyes, blinking, waking up on my own to an empty room.

I look at the sheet and blanket covering me, the outline of my legs and feet underneath. I wiggle my toes. Sunlight spills through the window and fills the room. The shadows from the trees dance on the bed, over me. It takes me some effort to roll over and swing my legs out of bed.

I slip my feet into my slippers. The big toe on my left foot pokes out of the tiny hole at the end of the slipper, as if the slippers have shrunk overnight. That can't be. I pull on them, trying to stretch them, but no matter how I position my foot, the slipper feels tighter.

I feel a pang of guilt, stressed that I haven't done enough work on Hilbert's portrait. Shelley wants us to stay productive, to work every day, to produce. It keeps us young and gives us a purpose. I need to get back to it today. I shouldn't waste the morning sleeping in like I have.

_____

I should get dressed. I should eat. I should paint.

There it is, the portrait of Hilbert, sitting on my desk, incomplete. How did it get on my desk? I walk closer to it, putting my cardigan on over my nightie. When did I last work on it? It looks . . . different. He looks different.

I feel goose bumps on my arms and then someone's stare locking on to me from behind. I swivel around, but there's no one else here. I'm alone.

I open my dresser drawer. I find the napkin I brought back from dinner last night and unwrap it. Inside are the two pieces of carrot. There is a tiny, dark patch of mold starting to grow on one of the carrots. I close the napkin and drop it in the garbage and sit on the bed.

"Morning, Penny," Jack says, walking in.

I look at Jack, trying to decide what to say. What should I tell him? Should I tell him I'm starting to understand what's actually happening here? That I'm starting to realize the extent of Shelley's infatuation with living and production? Doing it together. Just like a forest. All the same. Linked. It's happening here. Inside. With us. Within us.

Jack sits down on the bed beside me.

"I was in my same apartment for more than fifty years," I say. "I had friends over during that time, for meals and parties, but most of the time it was just me and him. I didn't want to have children. He did. We argued about it. Once, we had a huge fight. It's becoming hard to remember most of it."

"I know what that's like. That's why a place like this is right for both of us. Forgetting the past isn't always the worst thing."

"Doesn't it scare you? Not being able to remember parts of your life?"

"I would be more scared if I had to remember everything, all the time," he says. "Shelley believed enough to give me a chance when I'd used up a lot of chances already. It was a fresh start for me. Just like it was when you got here. We both are lucky to be part of this."

"This?"

"This house," he says. "Six Cedars."

1—2—3—4—5—6.

"What do you know about the forest out there?"

"It's very peaceful," he says.

"You see, now you sound like Shelley. I want to know about it.

How big is it? What else is out there? Does it surround the entire house? Does it go on forever? I feel like I can see trees from every window. I never get to be out there. Do you?"

"Why are you asking me all this, Penny?"

"Tell me! What's outside this house?"

"Calm down, please. I don't know what's wrong with you today. You're agitated."

I close my eyes, take a few breaths. I open them and look Jack in the eye. I can feel a sharp ache in my head.

"What does she want? What is she trying to do with us?"

"I like you, Penny. I really do. You have a spark. Things feel different since you've been around. Different for me. But I can't risk losing what I have here. She's right. I have nothing else."

Jack looks back over his shoulder before speaking.

"You're protected here from all the dangers of being an elderly woman, okay? You're taken care of, and you'll never be alone again. I promise."

Jack stands, touches me on the shoulder, pats it, and walks out.

Jack is gone, but I keep replaying what he said, that I'll never be alone again, that I'm being protected from being an elderly woman. That's what he said. Did he also say that forgetting is good?

But at what cost? At what cost am I being protected from my age?

I want to remember how much fun we had in our apartment. I never thought about what he was going to be like in middle age, in late middle age, as an old man. I never thought about how his desires would wane over time while his traits and mannerisms would intensify. As passions decrease, character is revealed.

I get up, and go looking for Jack. He can't be far away. He just left my room. He's wrong when he said he has nothing else.

I get to the common room and find Ruth sitting alone, watching the TV.

There's an old movie playing on the TV. I stand and watch it. I know it. I know it well. I remember seeing it for the first time in the theater. The cinema was full that night. I had popcorn with butter. I can smell it. I can feel how greasy my fingers would get, how I would lick the butter off them one at a time. And a large soda. It's *Thelma & Louise*. Ruth is watching intently. Her mouth is actually moving to the dialogue of the film. She must love it, too, as I do. I've seen this film so many times. Ruth knows it by heart.

They both die at the end of the movie. I loved that. I really love how the movie ends. It was the only way to end it in a satisfying way. They got out.

Ruth doesn't miss a line. It's mesmerizing to watch her watch the movie. As I look from her to the movie and back again, I realize she's not reciting the movie line by line in English. She's doing it in French. She's translating as she watches. In real time.

"Tu es tres jolie," I whisper to her.

My eyes drift to a painting on the wall. A large one. There never used to be anything on that wall. I'm in here every day. How have I never noticed it? It's always been a blank wall. I step closer to it. I feel a prickling sensation underneath my skin.

I bring my hand to my mouth. It can't be. It's one of his! I remember when he finished it. It had taken him so long. He was so invested in it. He was moody right up until he finished it. It never sold and despite it being his favorite, he said he wasn't surprised it never sold. He was fine with the fact that no one else would be able to see what he'd done, because it was his most personal.

Now here it is, hanging on the wall in front of me. I feel dizzy, sick. I have to put a hand on the wall to steady myself. I feel like I might fall over.

There's something on my leg. A cat is brushing against my ankle. It's hesitant at first, but slowly it becomes more aggressive, scratching at my leg. I shake my leg to get it off.

"Stop," I say. "Not now!"

But it won't stop. It bites at my slippers and nips my foot.

"Ouch!"

Suddenly, something spooks the cat. It darts down the hall. I bend and rub the spot it bit on my foot. Short of breath, I sit down to rest in the chair that's closest to me. I close my eyes.

J ack is lightly shaking my arm.

"Penny," he says.

I've fallen asleep in the common room. Ruth is gone. So is the cat. The TV is still on, but only static fuzz now. My mouth is so dry. I need water.

"Penny . . . please . . . wake up," he says.

He shakes my arm again. He looks rattled.

"I've been thinking more about what you said, and I have to tell you something. I have to be fast."

I open my eyes as wide as possible, focusing on his face. I'm dreaming. But I feel his hand on my arm. No, I was dreaming, before, but this is real. Jack. He's right in front of me, touching me, frantic.

"Penny!" he says again. "This place is her life's work. She believes in it. She's made it a community. She has all the control and can't risk any disruptions. She wants to understand more about how to live longer. The only thing that scares her is getting old and—"

We both hear a noise. Jack puts a finger to his lips.

"That's her," he says. "I have to go. You can't say anything to her about us talking like this."

I know what else he wants to say to me, just from the look in his eyes: *You're right, you've always been right about what she's doing to you. She's keeping you alive. All of you.*

Without another word, he abruptly turns and leaves the room.

Exhausted, confused, I close my eyes and rest my head against the back of the chair.

Footsteps in the hallway. Not leaving but coming toward the room. I was asleep in the chair. I want it to be Jack. To tell me more, to explain. But it's not him.

High heels. It's her.

"Napping in your favorite spot," Shelley says as she steps into the room. "I know how much you like the view in here."

Do I have a favorite spot? I have to clear my throat before I speak.

"What about that one?" I ask, pointing at a small chair against the wall.

"That chair?"

"Yes."

"There's nothing to look at if you sit there. You love your window seat. You can see the trees."

Have I ever sat here before?

I've always had vibrant dreams. Even as a young child. I've dreamed about colors. I have many small, short dreams. Restless dreams. Plotless dreams. Now, as an old woman I dream of the tall trees behind the residence, the ones with no leaves, standing in unison, swaying slightly, huddled together for warmth.

"I want to go outside."

Her expression changes. Not dramatically, but I notice.

"We have all these beautiful windows to provide as much light as possible. I don't want to upset you, but I think you're having a bit of a memory blip."

No, I think. I'm not having a memory blip. I'm just realizing I haven't been outside in days, not since I've moved in. I used to always go for walks, even in the coldest weather. I loved feeling the air on my face. I didn't care if my feet got wet in the rain. I can remember all of that.

"The forest, Penny. The cliffs. It's treacherous and snowy out there," she says. "And then with Gorky getting out last week."

"Gorky?"

"The cat. You picked his name. He died, remember? He got outside and froze to death. It was awful. You'll feel better after you rest, Penny."

"What? The cat didn't die!"

I look down to my foot, where he bit me. He bit me, but there's no cut. The skin is clear. I can feel the tears now on my cheeks. They've been building behind my eyes for hours, days.

Shelley touches my shoulder.

"Have a nap," she says, and walks out of the room.

Once she's gone, I turn and see that Hilbert is sitting beside me. Has he been here the whole time? He hasn't said anything. I'm still crying, but I feel a wave of relief at the sight of him.

He's working on the puzzle again, the one we started in his room, of the trees. How did it get in here? He's fixated on it. He's almost finished it.

"We can't go out there," he says looking up.

I see his face, his eyes. He's not looking well. He looks feeble and weak.

"Why, Hilbert? Why not?"

"It's dangerous. This is where we have to be." His voice is strained.

"Do you ever get any visitors?" I ask.

Hilbert looks down into his hands, as if he's wondering to whom they belong to.

"At home we have visitors. All the time," he says, looking up. "We have dinner parties and we listen to music and we all drink wine until very late. Sometimes we try to speak French together."

"What? No, Hilbert!" I say. "That was me. Not you."

"We need more time," he says. "We all do. Everyone does."

He closes his eyes, leaning back in his chair. With his eyes still closed, he speaks meekly, more to himself.

"Pando," he mutters. "Pando, from the puzzle."

"What, Hilbert? What's that?"

"Pando," he repeats flatly, closing his eyes. "'I spread.' In Latin, Pando means 'I spread.'"

I get up slowly and remove the slipper off Hilbert's right foot. It's hard because of the tremor in my hand. I'm horrified to see, just like mine, his toenails are long and jagged, as if they haven't been trimmed in weeks. I replace the slipper and stand up.

"Where are you going?" he asks.

"To look for something," I say. "You stay here."

I walk into the hallway, turning right, feeling the wall beside me as I walk.

As I pass the dining room, I catch a glimpse of Jack cleaning up. I've stumbled across a typical moment of his workday. I watch him for a minute from the shadows. I wait until there's no one around and head over to the side table where he was standing. There's a pamphlet, folded in half. I pick it up. There's a photo of . . . me.

In the photo, I'm so much younger. I'm smiling. It's strange to see it. I have no recollection of it.

I open the pamphlet and start to read aloud:

> *In her ninety-second year, Penny passed peacefully at Six Cedars Residence surrounded by her caring staff. She leaves behind her stunning art collection and all of her friends at the residence. Over the years, the staff and residents at Six*

Cedars loved Penny like family. A visitation was held at the residence, followed by a celebration of her life. Penny will be dearly missed.

I feel my legs threatening to give out from under me.

I drop the paper onto the table and cover my mouth with both hands. What is this? I feel a sharp pain in my head again—a deep, throbbing ache behind my eyes. I feel like I might be sick. I lean over, but nothing comes out, only a thin trail of bile and saliva.

What is going on? What's happening here? What are they doing to us?

She'll send this out, and people will believe it. She'll send it to Mike. He'll believe I'm gone, but I won't be. I'll be here with her.

What has she done to me?

I need to get back to my room, to be alone, to think. I need to hide. From her.

t's taking me longer than it should. I walk down the hallway that leads to my room, but this time, it doesn't. It leads to another hallway, so I turn right and follow it around. It keeps going around, so at some point I stop.

I turn back.

This house is a maze. These hallways aren't what they appear to be. They're longer. Or shorter, depending on the day. They're narrow at night, wider in the morning. They change, these hallways, depending on who is walking them and at what point in their life they're in them.

I go the other way when I get back to the last hall. It's longer than it's ever been, altered since yesterday. It's the same hallway. I recognize it, but it's longer.

I turn back once more and make another turn, left this time, before I get back to my door.

I go inside, to my bathroom. I close the door. I can't get that pamphlet out of my mind. I wasn't supposed to see it. Now it's all I can see.

Over the years, the staff and residents at Six Cedars loved Penny like family.

Over the years . . .

Years . . .

How long have I been here? It's only been four days. I don't understand.

I'm sweating, splashing cold water over my face. I dry my face with the towel, trying to steady my hands. I move to the toilet. I hold my nightgown up off the floor. I sit to pee.

When finished, as I'm standing up, I flush. Something in the toilet catches my eye. I lean over, trying to see before the swirling water takes it away—subtle movement in the water, tiny particles. Are they alive?

Shocked, I step back, slamming the lid shut.

I scream. I don't hear any sound from my mouth, but I'm screaming.

Where am I?

243

What am I doing here?

H

ow long have I been here?

I flush the toilet for a second time and wait for the tank to fill. I do it again, and again, and again.

When I walk out into my room, she's there. Shelley. Her hair and makeup are immaculate. She's gorgeous. She's in her red dress and wearing her latex gloves.

"Hi, Penny, dear," she says. "Just getting your room cleaned up."

She's holding a long feather duster and is slowly moving around the room, dusting various surfaces and objects. There's also a cleaning bucket by the bed. I walk over and tap the bucket with my foot. The dark, greasy water ripples.

"Have a seat. I'll be done soon."

"My room is clean," I say, sitting down on my bed.

"But it won't stay clean. It never does. Not when we live in it."

"I saw . . ."

But I hesitate, unsure if I should say anything about the pamphlet.

She dusts the framed photo on my dresser.

"What did you see?"

"A pamphlet. An announcement about my death. I saw it."

"I'm sorry, Penny. Jack shouldn't have left that lying around. That must have been strange to see it."

I feel like my blood is boiling. How dare they!

"Why would that be written already? You're sending it to people so they think I'm dead!" I say. "So they won't ask about me. So you can keep me here for as long as you want!"

"Who are you expecting to ask about you? Has Mike called to check in? Has he visited? We're not sending it to anyone, Penny. I'm sorry, but there's no one to send a pamphlet to."

This stops me in my tracks.

"The truth is your partner wrote that before he died," she says. "It was his way of helping and trying to make sure everything would be done to a high standard. He tried to take care of everything. He told me that's what you would want. You were never meant to see that. That's Jack's fault for leaving it out."

"Where's Jack?" I ask.

She stops, puts the duster down.

"Penny, please. You're not listening to me."

"What are you trying to do to us?" I ask. "You can't force us to live this way. You can't!"

"Do you know what catabolic means, Penny?"

"No," I say.

"It means destructive metabolism. When a delicate ecosystem—like the one here at Six Cedars, where we all live together—is created, each life helps sustain the life of another. We all benefit from it. We give each other life. That's how we live here."

She steps closer.

"So each life is then dependent on the other. We need each other, Penny. We all have to fit in."

I look down at my hands; it's impossible how wrinkled and veiny they've become, almost useless. It's what everyone wants: to feel younger and to have more time.

"When a violin string is plucked, another string might vibrate in sympathy even though it's not touched," she says. "Human beings are the same. The more you can let go of the past, the more you can relax, the better off you'll be here. You don't have to worry about going back. You'll always be here with us."

There's a full glass of water on my bedside table, and I consider taking a sip to quench my heavy thirst. But instead, feeling too weary, I lie down on my side.

"Penny, you lived with him for so many years."

"Pardon me?"

Shelley turns the framed photo on the dresser back around to face me. Him. The man I spent so much time with. The man who could only see the world in one way, from one perspective. The man who needed so desperately to fit in.

"This was the spot you picked to come to, and he made sure you'd be taken care of for as long as possible. You should be grateful for all the extra time you're getting, Penny. Time he didn't get."

I close my eyes and pull my pillow to my chest. I shut my eyes. I don't want to see her anymore. I can still hear her moving around, and then nothing for a bit, until she speaks.

"People give up on themselves much too easily. There's no reason we can't keep striving to do more."

As she leaves, she switches off the light with a click. Silence.

"No," I say to the empty room. "You're wrong. We just can't accept letting go."

Pitch darkness. It's so dark I can't see the wall or dresser from the bed. It's so dark it's hard to see my hand as I hold it in front of my face. It must be the middle of the night, yet I'm wide awake.

I reach for the glass of water on the bedside table, but the glass is empty. There are dried paint flecks on my hand. When was I painting? I swing my legs out of bed, slipping my feet into my slippers. They must have stretched, as they don't feel as snug.

In the hall, I'm moving almost against my will, as if I'm being led. I end up at the front entrance, at the stairwell. I'm so tired from the walk, physically drained, that I rest my head against the wall before I bend down to look at the framed picture there. Near the bottom, I see it—the spot where I'd made that single scratch last night with my hairpin.

But now there are many scratches, at least forty, fifty, too many to count. My heart is thrashing in my chest. I can't slow it down. My breath, too, is coming in short, fast gulps. The rest of me, my arms, my legs, my eyes, are frozen. I can't move.

I look down the stairs. Have I ever been there? Should I go down? I don't want to. I don't want to see what's down there. But if I'm going to understand this house and what's happening to us, then I have to. I have to see for myself.

I'm gripping the banister for dear life, putting both feet on each step as I descend. I hear a thud, which causes me to stop on the last step. I hear it again. It sounds more like a groaning. I follow it, the sound, the feeling, despite my fear. I enter the first room I see, a doorway appearing on my left. It's hard to see in the blackness. There's almost no light, and what little there is, I can't tell the source.

Two steps in, my slipper catches and I almost fall from a bag lying on the floor. I look down and see there are several bags all of similar size. They look like pillowcases. I see now there are many bags piled up around the room. What kind of room is this? A closet? A storage room? I can't tell what is above me or where I am in proximity to my own room.

I pick up the bag that tripped me. I open it at the top. I can't see what's inside. So I reach my hand in hesitantly until I can touch the contents. I slowly remove a handful of soft fibers.

I bring it up to my face. I think I'm holding . . . hair.

As soon as I recognize what it is, I drop it and wipe my hand on my leg. I'm biting my bottom lip so hard I can taste blood as I open a second bag, dumping its contents onto the floor. It's filled with what must be nail clippings. I start to cough. I collapse in on myself, falling into the wall.

There are many bags, too many to count. How long have they been there? How long have I been here? They are filled with years' worth of hair and nail clippings.

I push the bags at my feet aside, leaving the room, and walk toward where the sound is coming from. There's a single bed at the far end of the room. There's nothing else in the room. I go toward it. There's a horizontal shape on the bed that is not moving. When I'm about halfway, whatever is on the bed makes the sound I've been hearing: a deep exhale, a sigh.

I stop, wondering if I should continue. I look back to the stairs. When I reach the bedside, I can tell it's a person. It's Hilbert. When did I last see him? When did we last speak? My heart is racing, pumping at the sight of him.

There are several glowing lamps around him, humidifiers, I think, and a fan.

He looks in bad shape.

"Hilbert? Are you okay?"

He moans. "It's cold," he says. His voice is fragile.

It's hard to see clearly in the shadows. I pull the covers up around him, trying to warm him. It looks like the fungus has spread over more of his body. His face and hands appear covered. His poor hands and fingers look crooked, deformed.

"Oh no, no, what happened? It's me—Penny. I've been looking for you everywhere. This can't be. What's happened to you?"

I need some light, I need to see him better, clearer. "What did she do to you?" I ask.

He's trying to tell me something, but he keeps stopping before any words come out. I sit down on the side of the bed. He puts his hand on mine. Its weight is comforting but also awkward. It's not the hand that I know.

"I'm scared. . . . I'm going to help you. . . . I promise."

"There's still more work to do," he says. "She wants us to keep working. We should be working. But I'm tired."

"No," I say. "You don't have to now. Not anymore."

"A lie is never truly scary," he says. "Because it's a lie."

"What's the lie this time?"

"This lie is one about life, that we need more of it, that we need to be more productive, produce more, that it has to be longer, that death is the enemy. It's not true. Infinity is a breathtaking mystery, or so I used to believe. Now I know it's not. Infinity is stagnant. It doesn't expand. It can't. It's just immeasurable. It's not a mystery, it's simply endless."

I smooth a stray piece of hair from his forehead.

"What can we do?"

"We're here. We have no choice now," he says.

I rub the back of his hand with my free one, then I lean in and kiss it. When I straighten, I hear movement above us, perhaps footsteps.

"Shelley wants what everyone wants," he replies. "What does everyone always say they want? What does everyone think they want? More. But it's not hard to see that more time would eventually become—"

"The worst thing," I say, finishing his thought. "Hell."

"Hell," he repeats.

That's when I realize what I have to do. Right now. Finally. I know. It's clear.

"I'm going to help you," I say. "I'm going to help all of us."

I hug him. As hard as I can.

"I wish I'd known you sooner," he says, "for longer."

"We know each other right now."

"You're here with me right now."

"Yes, and that's enough."

"We have helped each other," he says.

"Yes, but I have to do this on my own," I say.

"So do I," he says.

I hold the hug and feel his hand patting my back.

"Goldbach's conjecture, I finally remember it," he says, as I'm standing to go. "And I want to make sure I tell you. It's important: For every even number n>2, there exist two prime numbers p_1

and p_2 such that we can write: $p\_1 + p\_2 = n$ ... Numbers and letters, you see? We need both, Penny."

I go to him, kiss him softly on the forehead. I feel the thinness of his skin with my lips. I let my forehead rest against his. "You don't have to remember that anymore," I say. "You've done all the work you need to do."

"I've always liked the shape of your cheek," he says.

As gently as I can, I rub my cheek against his. I feel his stubble, holding it for a moment. Then I pull away, turn away from him, and leave.

've lost track of how long I've been here, walking these deceptive halls, in this constricting house, the days, the hours, the minutes, the seconds. I'm lying in bed, but I can't fall asleep. My mind is racing. Someone is in the room with me. I feel like someone else.

I want Hilbert to rest.

There are only four residents here. It's full, but only four of us. There must be more rooms in a house this size. There are only two people who work here. I see all the same people every day. I go from my room to eat, to sit, to eat, back to my room, to sleep, to wake, to eat. Over and over. We all do. We all do the same things. We're told the same things. We eat the same things.

"Is someone there?" I call to the dark room.

I get up, flip on the light. I wait, listening. I walk to my desk, back to bed, lie down. I get up again, walk around the room. I go into the bathroom. I drink some water out of my cupped hands.

I can't fall asleep, so I put on my noise-canceling headphones. Once I turn them on, there's no sound at all. I feel the pressure on my bladder after the water. I get back up, put my cardigan on, headphones still on, and sit on the toilet.

I stand, flush the toilet, which I can't hear, and go back to bed. I keep my sweater on against the chill.

The room is dark. It's not until I'm almost asleep that I realize what was different in the bathroom. The shower curtain was drawn across the shower. I always leave it open so I can see inside. But it was closed tonight. I don't want to go back and check it yet again.

I need to rest, to sleep.

A tall, thin, silver pole beside my bed. It's the first thing I see in the early-morning light. An IV pole, with a clear bag of fluid hanging from it. This isn't a hospital. It's a house. It's a residence. It's supposed to be a home. My home. I have the sensation of insects crawling all over me as I follow the IV line from the bag, which leads to me. I push my sleeve up to see where it enters the back of my arm. The fluid is going into me.

My chest feels heavy, tight. It's too late now. She's putting something inside me. She never told me about it. She must have put it in Hilbert, too. And Ruth. And Pete. All of us. The same thing.

I feel around where the line goes into my arm. It's covered in see-through tape, which I peel off. I close my eyes and pull the line out, as fast as I can.

Now I'm standing in the hall.

Now I'm walking.

Now I'm looking for her. Shelley.

Now I'm at the bottom of the staircase. I can hear talking coming from another room on the floor above. I don't need to go down but up. I'm stepping carefully, hoping to remain silent, up the stairs.

There's a door I've never seen leading into a room I've never been in. A bright, white, antiseptic light spills from the room. I hear them talking.

"We can't stop it now."

"I know that." A man's voice. Is there someone else here? Is it Jack?

"How do you feel?" he asks.

"I feel great."

"You're looking very well," he says.

"It took longer than I thought it would," she says.

I lean closer, trying to see more through the open door, but I can't.

"I guess because she's the last, I hoped it was going to be easier with Penny."

"I did, too."

"But ease isn't why we're here."

Finally, I'm able to see more, only shadows, but I can tell what it is. It's the shadows of more IV lines, moving along the floor like snakes, all together. I count, one—two—three—four lines.

I turn back and start down the stairs.

walk. I walk as best I can. I sit and rest. I walk along the hallway some more.

I end up in the common room, the early-morning light, almost blue in color, not full sun yet. This has always been my favorite time of day because it doesn't last. I would go to the park just for this magical hour. It's so easy to miss. Everyone takes it for granted every single day they wake up. It's only a moment. It's magical, it's beautiful.

I look out. I've never put my hand on these windows. I've never touched them.

I walk in between the barriers of the couch, side tables, and plants. I'm directly in front of the massive windows. When I'm this close to them, the dimensions feel even bigger than I thought they were. Taller and wider. I've never been so close to these windows. I feel smaller. It looks so cold out there. There are so many trees out there, so many that we'll only ever be able to see a tiny part of the forest. A fraction.

A glimmer of light catches my eye, near the bottom of the window. I bend down. There's a spot on the window that's slightly brighter. I touch it. It doesn't feel the way I'm expecting it will. It's softer. I push my finger harder against it. It . . . gives. It moves slightly. Its resistance is elastic.

I retrieve a piece from the Pando puzzle that's sitting on the table near me. Pando is Latin for "I spread." He told me that. Hilbert. I have to break it apart and I use it to push, using all the force I can muster, into the window. The glass bends like a taut sheet, and the piece I'm holding ends up poking right through. It doesn't shatter like glass should but creates a tiny hole.

I feel like the room is spinning. I don't understand. The floor isn't steady under my feet.

I put my eye directly up to the opening and look through it. Instead of the forest, it's another hallway, similar to the hallway outside my room. The difference is obvious, but I can't decipher it. And then I realize. It's the carpet. I know this carpet.

It's the carpet I had in my old apartment.

The hole is too small to see much else, but I can make out some lights and other equipment. I see a violin. A French dictionary. Stacks of blue graph paper and a pencil. Several blank canvases. My eye and cheek are pressed right against the hole when I feel the sensation of being grabbed from behind. Something has me, is holding on to me. I feel a surge of pure panic before everything goes blank.

I'm startled awake by a light touch on my shoulder.

I blink, try to focus. There's nothing to see. I hear a voice.

"Penny," Jack whispers, stepping closer to my bed.

I open my eyes wider. He looks at me affectionately. He's tense, skittish.

"What happened?" I ask. "I'm scared."

"You had another nightmare. You were screaming."

I focus on my breathing. In and out, in and out.

"Why am I still here? I don't think I should be."

"Penny . . ."

"Are you keeping me . . . alive? All of us?"

"Oh, Penny."

Again, he touches my shoulder. "I'm sorry," he says. "I'm not a good person."

"You are," I say. "I think you are."

"I wish I'd been better. I made a lot of mistakes."

"You've been kind to me," I say.

"I came here because I had nothing and needed to work. She told me, 'What's more important to life than living?' I thought she was smart and caring."

His face is ruddy and gaunt.

"Please tell me! Right now! What's inside this house? What's outside?" I ask. "The doors are locked."

"Of course they are."

"But . . ."

"You should be able to go outside. It's not right that you can't," he says.

He turns toward the door, as if he's heard something.

"Jack . . ."

He puts a finger to his lips.

"What's your biggest regret?" I ask.

"I haven't lived my full life yet, so I can't say. It depends how long I have."

"I remember a lady outside my apartment building once said: 'You're going to hell when you die.' She yelled it at me. 'You're going to hell!' That seemed so scary in that moment, when I was a young woman, to hear someone say *when you die*. To think about your own death, dying, how close it is for everyone. But now I know that's not the horrifying part."

"Isn't it?"

"No. Hilbert and I have been talking. The tragedy of life isn't that the end comes. That's the gift. Without an end, there's nothing. There's no meaning. Do you see? A moment isn't a moment. A moment is an eternity. A moment should mean something. It should be everything."

His eyes are wet, but he doesn't look sad. He doesn't move for some time. He turns his head, looks down at my bedside table, and I follow his eyes to a single piece of paper and pencil.

"You're right," he says.

He picks up the paper and pencil, scribbles something on it, then puts the pencil and paper back down on the table.

"For you," he says, touching my arm. "I know how much you like the fresh air."

He walks out without looking back.

I pick up paper. On one side is an old note I'd written for myself.

You loved talking with Hilbert.

I turn the paper over and look at the message Jack has just written for me.

6 – 7 – 8 – 8 – 7

"And you just had a bad dream, Penny. Are you okay?"

It's her, Shelley, standing by my bed, leaning over me.

"Get away from me," I say. "Don't touch me."

I open my eyes as wide as I can, taking her in.

"I know what's true," I say.

"Please, Penny. This isn't helping."

"Open my window! You can't. Because the windows are fake. They aren't real."

"What are you talking about?"

"I know they aren't real. You can't open them."

Shelley walks over to the window, opens it, puts her long arm outside.

"It's cold out there. Can I close it, please? Penny?"

"I want to see Jack do it."

"Jack's not here right now."

"What? What do you mean? What was that thing doing in my arm?"

"That thing, as you call it, is important. You need it. You were getting dehydrated. You've had it for six months. I keep hoping you'll get used to it."

I feel the color drain from my face.

"I've never seen it until this morning."

"Do you know why you're here? Why you're not still living in your apartment?"

"Because I'm so old. And now you're using me. All of us."

"Because you're unwell, Penny, and you need our help. And, sometimes, like today, you really forget things, and then you get confused and scared and upset."

"Why aren't you telling me the truth?"

"The truth is you are cared for and well looked after. You're thriving here."

"Where's Hilbert? Tell me where you've taken him."

"Hilbert hasn't been feeling well. He's resting."

"You hurt him. You're keeping him alive . . . you're doing it to all of us."

She breaks eye contact for a moment. She's trying to compose herself. "It's good that you care about your friend Hilbert. But you need to stop worrying, Penny. I can still remember your first day. You and Hilbert hit it off right away."

"But I've only just moved in. I'm new."

She tilts her head, smiles. "You can't use that term forever. Not when you've been living here for over three years, Penny."

I hear the words. But I don't believe them. This can't be true. I just moved in.

"You're lying! Where's Jack? Where's Hilbert?"

"Jack has the day off."

I don't say anything.

"Would you like to see Hilbert? You just have to promise not to disturb him."

"I want to see him."

"Okay, come on, I'll take you to him. Let's go."

She helps me with my IV.

S helley opens Hilbert's door and waits for me to enter first.

I see him. He's there. Right in front of me. He's lying in his bed, asleep. He's tucked in tightly, the covers up to his chin. He's unshaven. I've never seen him with such long whiskers and his hair disheveled. As I get closer, I reach out and pick up the book on his bedside, *Noncommutative Geometry and Number Theory: Where Arithmetic Meets Geometry and Physics*. He's written a few lines in pencil on the margin of the page it's open to.

Ask Penny if she finds it comforting that there are mathematical proofs of impossibility. Example: Trisecting an angle. Divide any angle into three equal parts.

My chest feels warm as I close the book and set it beside his bed.

"You see," Shelley says quietly. "He's peaceful and content."

I look at him. He's amazing. He's wonderful. I don't know where he was born, or what his childhood was like. But I feel a deep affection for him as I stand by his bedside. He's a gentle man. He always was, I'm sure of that.

"I saw him just last night. He was very unwell."

"I don't know what you mean, Penny. You're seeing him right now, as he is."

I reach out to touch him, but she stops me, grabbing my hand.

"No, don't. He needs to rest."

I pull my hand back. "It's just, I'm sure of it. He was . . ."

I trail off.

"We're hoping he'll be up for tonight."

"Tonight?"

"The party!"

"You keep talking about a party . . ."

"It's not your fault. It's hard to remember all the details. You love our parties. Every time we have one, you tire yourself out dancing."

She pulls me in and hugs me. My face is buried in her shoulder for what feels like a long time. She's hugging me the way my father used to hug me when my feelings were hurt.

"But I'm new here," I say.

"Oh, Penny. Tonight's your big night."

"My big night?"

She releases me from the hug. I see a thin IV line running out from under Hilbert's blanket into a bag hanging by his bed.

"Tonight's your first-ever show! It's your opening."

I've never had a show. I've never had an opening, or displayed my work publicly. Not once. Not ever.

"Maybe I'll show you something," she says. "A sneak peek."

"Show me what?"

"I was hoping I wouldn't have to, not until tonight."

"Show me what?" I repeat.

"Your paintings. You've become so prolific. It's very impressive."

She walks out to the hall, leaving me alone with Hilbert. I move closer to him. I want to touch him, to take the covers off him, make sure his arms and hands are intact, but as I take hold of his hand, Shelley comes back carrying a box. She opens the lid. She puts the box on the floor.

"Here, have a look. I'm just about to set them up."

I release Hilbert's hand and reach into the box she's holding. I pull out several canvases. Each is a painting.

"They're marvelous," she says.

It's unmistakable. It is my work.

"There are more," she says.

There must be thirty or forty paintings in this box. It would take years to paint them all. None are the same. All portraits. Of Pete, Ruth, and Hilbert. They're incomplete. She doesn't notice. But I do. A small detail here and there. Unfinished.

I feel like I've been drained of blood. I can't speak. I have nothing to say. I feel deflated. I feel old.

"We're so proud of you and your work, Penny, and we can't wait to showcase it tonight at the party. You're looking tired. It's your eyes. Let's get you back to your room for a nap."

There are so many trees outside this house, so many you could never know them all, but each one is there. Each one counts. I noticed them on my first day, before I saw the inside of the house, before I met the others.

I'm standing beside Hilbert's bed. He's awake. We're not talking. We don't need to.

I'm holding his hand one more time before I go.

The common room is prepared for a party, an opening. I'm not there, but that doesn't matter. I can see it perfectly with my eyes closed. All of it. Everything. They're all there. Balloons, and streamers, and punch. The carpet has been vacuumed, the windows washed. Pete tuning his violin. Ruth is reciting Latin, too, rather than French.

What I've done is enough. It's beautiful only because there's an end. There are so many things we can just let go. Tant de choses à laisser aller.

I'm in my bed, but I'll go outside. They don't know it yet, but they'll get to go out, too, because of me. It's a gift. It's my gift to them. Pete doesn't have to play anymore. Ruth can put her French dictionary back on the shelf. Hilbert can put down his pencil; he doesn't need any more blue graph paper.

We do not all blend together. We are not ruined, helpless, a burden. We are not the elderly. We are not old people. Now, still, we're unique. Distinct. Regardless of what we've produced or what happens to our bodies. We each have our own memories and experiences, even if they've been lost and forgotten.

They, we, all of us can finally rest.

'm not in my bed anymore. I've already snuck away, but I can still see: Shelley walking down the hall in her high heels, walking until she reaches my room. She enters straightaway, without speaking. My shape, my outline, is there, lying in the bed, under the covers.

She glances up toward the ceiling, and when she does, her legs give out from under her. She must sit down. She's seeing it for the first time. My actual work. All that I've done. A massive mural painted on the ceiling of my room that stretches into the bathroom and the hallway to the common room. Its scale is immense. Unthinkable. I can't say how long it's taken me.

It will spread to them. All of them. To Ruth and Pete. Hilbert. It will spread to Jack. And to Shelley.

I hope she feels something. I hope it comforts her.

My freshly painted red nails press each button on the keypad at the Six Cedars entrance.

6—7—8—8—7 or O—R—T—U—S.

Numbers and letters.

The door clicks and opens.

I'm nervous; I'm afraid. It's so cold.

I look back once. Then I go. I step outside.

'm walking barefoot, wearing only my nightgown as I follow a stone path into the trees, heading toward the dense forest. It's snowy, but I don't feel the bite of cold. The ground is steep and harsh. My feet are pale. I have makeup on. For the opening.

I hear the ringing of an alarm. I see the cat sitting beside a small tree. I walk over, bend down, and scratch behind its ears. Suddenly, everything goes completely quiet, as if I'm wearing the noise-canceling headphones.

But I'm not. I'm not wearing any headphones.

The quiet is everywhere, around and inside of me.

I continue walking amid the trees until I reach the edge of the forest where the terrain has eroded, until I'm standing atop a steep cliff. It's so high. I love the light at this time of the morning. It never lasts long.

I move cautiously toward the edge. Butterflies fill my stomach. I peer over but can't see anything. I feel the air, the wind. For a moment everything is still. I close my eyes. I feel myself rise off the ground, fall through the air. I'm hurtling at great speed, or maybe, for a moment, I'm floating.

In her ninety-second year, Penny passed peacefully at Six Cedars Residence surrounded by her caring staff. She leaves behind her stunning art collection and all of her friends at the residence. Over the years, the staff and residents at Six Cedars loved Penny like family. A visitation was held at the residence, followed by a celebration of her life. Penny will be dearly missed.

ACKNOWLEDGMENTS

My grandma moved into a long term care facility the year she turned one hundred. We spent a lot of time there with her, where she lived for almost two years, until she passed away. I want to thank all PSW's, nurses, staff, volunteers, and all who work and help at long term care facilities. Thank you.

ABOUT THE AUTHOR

Iain Reid is the author of four previous books, including his *New York Times*–bestselling debut novel *I'm Thinking of Ending Things*, which has been translated into more than twenty languages. Oscar-winner Charlie Kaufman wrote and directed the film adaptation for Netflix. His second novel, *Foe*, is being adapted for film, starring Saoirse Ronan, with Reid cowriting the screenplay. His latest novel is *We Spread*. Reid lives in Ontario, Canada.